FULL FURY

Monday, Tuesday, Wednesday, and Thursday. Dave took up his first case on Monday, and, in the space of four days, had to complete it before he got married on Friday and could go away on honeymoon.

Neville Gaines had been hanged twelve years before for shooting and killing farmer Andy Paterson. What was to be gained by going over the case again? Were there two guns used or just the one – and what significance did this have now? Much is discovered before the conclusion and few escape unscathed in this investigation.

FULL FURY

Roger Ormerod

·BLACK·
DAGGER
·CRIME·

c-\

First published 1975
by
Robert Hale and Company

This edition 2000 by Chivers Press
published by arrangement with
the author

ISBN 0 7540 8578 3

British Library Cataloguing in Publication Data available

Printed and bound in Great Britain by
Redwood Books, Trowbridge, Wiltshire

CHAPTER ONE

Perhaps there was something wrong with my smile. The thing called Troy levered his shoulders away from my wall and moved down on me. I didn't have time to shift from the desk as the cigar came stabbing down at my fingers. I fanned them, and a square inch of plastic top was permanently scarred.

And all I'd said to Finn was: 'What d'you do to make it talk?'

'There's an ashtray,' I said mildly, indicating a couple of pounds of glass, and Troy flicked it to the floor with one of the three fingers on his left hand.

That was just about the end of the visit, the closing pleasantries, you might say. Carter Finn's true business had been gracefully skirted. He stood up and called off his hired support with a movement of his eyes, and they moved to the door.

'Oh,' said Finn, 'to start you on your new career...' And he tossed the briefcase over. I caught it. 'An enquiry agent needs a briefcase.'

I stood at the window and watched them go. Troy glanced up for a moment and the day lost its charm. The car, I decided, was a big Rover.

It was a bad omen that my first client should have been Finn. If you could call him that. My office door had been open for a fortnight, and nobody had shown any interest. Then that morning I'd climbed the last of the stairs, opened the door, and there he was in the outer office. I don't think I registered shock; I simply led the way through.

I might have guessed Finn wouldn't be alone, but I hadn't spotted his goon, standing in the corner. Then somehow, by the time I'd got to my desk, he was easing apart two of my walls with his shoulders.

Finn looked round with contempt, then took the only chair I'd got in there. It creaked a little. He's a big man, broad with it. He smelt faintly of an after-shave that could have been deadly nightshade.

'I heard they finally threw you out,' he said patiently.

'You could say it was mutual.'

'Not what I heard.'

He was greying a little, I thought. How old would he be —fifty? But still aggressively active.

'A man in your position,' I told him, 'hears what people think you want to hear.'

He made the shishing noise that Finn used for a laugh. 'Oh come on, Mr Mallin. Would I be pleased that they'd pitched you out of the force?'

Would he? We'd never directly clashed, but there'd been some edgy moments.

'We found we didn't think on the same lines,' I told him.

'And now you've gone private?'

'I'm going.'

'But not busy?'

'Not busy,' I agreed.

There was a buzzer connected to the outer door, but I'd never yet heard it. There was a phone that I knew was working but it never rang for me.

'You ought to advertise,' he said placidly.

'I do.'

What the hell did he want from me? Anything I had to offer did not fit in with his background of clubs and gaming houses. Yet there was that new pigskin briefcase on his plump lap, and a keen, searching gleam in his eyes.

He said it was mild for March—you could almost smell the Spring in the air. I got up to look out of the dirty window. There was no sign of Spring on the asphalt below, but almost opposite was parked a big grey car that was probably Finn's. Something ugly was behind the wheel and had a pink paper spread over it. I agreed it was very mild for March.

'What you want to do,' he said, 'is let me have some of your visiting cards. I meet a lot of people.'

'I can't see your friends bringing me anything legal.'

Finn smiled. He had one of those soft, smooth faces that simply shine when they're pressed to it. There was talcum in the wrinkles spreading from his eyes. He was trying to be friendly, and nearly succeeded in hiding his viciousness. But he owed me no favours, and I certainly owed him none.

The smile was so surprising that I glanced at his nurse-maid to gauge the effect. He was smoking a small cigar, making no show-off attempt to appear bored, but calmly watching me. He knew his job. He'd remember me. A good lad. I looked away, feeling uneasy.

But in fact it was all too easy to toss insults at a man like Finn. You didn't have to worry about hurting him, and as he said from time to time, he couldn't lash back. Always calm and precise, Carter Finn. Always walking a legal tightrope.

'So you haven't got work for me.' I paused, but he didn't say he had. 'Then why have you come?'

He lifted his hands a few inches and spread them in appeal. 'Why else but to wish you luck?'

'I don't need your sort of luck.'

The lad in the corner moved and a shoe creaked. I

looked across in time to catch a frown, though whether at me or at his shoe I couldn't tell.

'I was driving past,' said Finn blandly, 'and I thought I'd drop in on David Mallin. They lost a good man when you resigned...'

'Resigned?' So he'd known.

'You should look us up, Mallin. Usually I'm at The Beeches. You're an honorary member. Did you know?'

I was not sure I wanted any connection with Finn's clubs, but I couldn't have said exactly why. When I'd been in the police we'd kept a sharp eye on him, but there'd never been anything we could put a finger on.

'I may look you up.' I tried it again. 'But no work?'

'I've got all the staff I need.'

All right, I nearly shouted, then why don't you go? He looked around at my filing cabinet and my desk. The cabinet was new, full of empty folders to take my case records. The desk was old. The drawers held my new pipe and a tin of tobacco, and a paperback I couldn't wait to get back to. There was a fancy calendar on the wall.

'You're in business on your own now,' he said. 'So brighten the place up. Look big, Mallin. Make a show. They want to give money to those who've already got plenty.'

His philosophy. With him it had certainly worked. A lot of money circulated round Carter Finn, and a good deal of it drifted into his bank accounts. That was a very expensive suit he was wearing. The pin in his silk tie would have kept me eating for a year.

'I'll do that,' I agreed readily. I nodded towards his helper. 'One you're breaking in?'

Finn looked at his protégé with affection. 'He's a likely lad. We call him Troy.'

We both stared at him. The square shoulders moved

with what might have been embarrassment. Not more than twenty, I thought, slim and fast. He was wearing a large-checked jacket in mustard and brown over a cream shirt with a red and gold tie, knotted large. Hair not too long, a wide brow with hard, dark and straight eyebrows, and tiny eyes, grey I thought, though he didn't show me much of them. If he'd smiled he might have been handsome. His mouth did something, but it didn't turn out as a smile. He moved his right hand across his lips, perhaps annoyed that they had done something, and there was a gold chain round his wrist.

I turned back to Finn. 'What d'you do to make it talk?' And that was when Troy decided he'd had enough of the cigar.

I turned away from the window and went to have a look at my wall calendar. It usually comforted me. March. A snow scene—the pessimists! A magpie on a low gate, with the fence shadows pink across the snow bank. But now it chilled me. I shivered, and decided there was nothing wrong with the calendar. It was me.

There was nothing you could definitely level against Carter Finn. He ran a number of successful and rather smart clubs on a strictly legal basis. Where he had gaming tables, they were rigidly honest. There was nothing wrong. So why the hell did he need so many ex-cons and crooks in his establishments?

I looked at his present. It was an expensive item, with double straps and a lock. He hadn't left me the keys, but when I looked inside they were there, way down beneath all the paperwork. I laid it all out on the desk to see exactly why Carter Finn had come to see me.

I was looking at a transcript of the trial of Neville Gaines, aged 48, for the murder of Andrew Paterson. There were photostats of the reports, day by day, in *The*

Times. There was also a photostat of the report of his execution. Pentonville. The 12th of March, twelve years ago. It was his anniversary today.

The only interest, as far as I could see, that Finn could have in the case was that he now operated from the house where Neville Gaines had lived—The Beeches.

Just because it was there, I sat down and read it through. It took me through seven pipes of tobacco and two pots of coffee from the Ramona opposite. Finn couldn't have known—my name never appeared in the papers—but it was only a matter of refreshing my memory. I'd been on the case. Well, not exactly on it, because I was a very young constable then, but I had been there. Det. Chief Inspector Crowshaw's driver, that was me.

But all the same I read it carefully, because I hadn't gone to the trial. Twice, as I say, I went across for coffee, mainly to try and get a clear sight of the man sitting behind the wheel of the car just along the street. He was there all afternoon. It was a red Mini Cooper with a black top and those matt black patches on the doors to impress you with the driver's technique. I didn't get my clear sight. The very pleasant March sun hit back at me from his windscreen.

As he didn't seem inclined to come up and see me, I phoned Elsa at about three. I'd thought I would find out how far things had gone with the arrangements, and at the same time I asked if she'd like to go out that evening.

'Evening dress stuff,' I said.

'I'll be too tired.' Her voice was tense. She was obviously working on it too hard, but I suppose it's always the same with weddings.

'You could do with the break,' I suggested.

'David, you simply don't realize...'

There was perhaps a criticism there. But I'd offered.

Really, I had. And she had said get off to your office, David, and let me get on with it. You'll gather she wasn't keen on the office.

'But you could manage it?'

'Oh—I suppose so.'

So we fixed it up, which meant I'd got to dig out the dinner jacket and press out a few wrinkles.

I locked away Neville Gaines and drove back to my place. The car was a Porsche that Elsa had given me for an engagement present. I felt good, driving it. I let the Mini tag along.

Up to that time I had not moved from my two and a bit rooms in the crescent. Now that there was an impending break between us I was feeling a sentimental liking for the place, even its pokiness. I put the kettle on and laid out two cups and saucers, and I was just pitching tea into the pot when the knock came at the door.

'Come in,' I shouted. 'It's open.'

He eased his way in cautiously, as though I might be lurking just out of sight with a cosh. His eyes swept the room. But I was alone. He closed the door behind him.

He would have been half-way through his twenties, a dark, shy-looking young man, a little shorter than I am. He had still got his huge sun glasses on. His hair was untidy, I suppose because it would be against his principles to drive with his window shut. His face was interesting. He was quick, sharp, his mouth moving, never still for a moment, expending expressions so fast that you never caught up. And nervous. His eyes flickered, caught me, hesitated, backed off. He was fiddling constantly with a pair of black driving gloves, half stuffing them into the pocket of his padded motoring coat, then pulling them out again.

'Sit down,' I said. 'The kettle's coming up.'

He sat with his knees together, perching the gloves on

them. After a moment he took off the glasses, and I saw that his eyes were grey and wide.

'It took you long enough,' I said.

There was very nearly a blush. 'You saw me?'

I looked at him solemnly. 'I'm a detective.'

It seemed to give him satisfaction, as though he'd set me a test and I'd passed with honour.

'I wanted to be sure,' he said at last.

'I've got an office you could have made sure in.'

He blinked. 'Your kettle's boiling.'

I made the tea. It was the Porsche that'd done it. He'd trust a man who ran such a car, not knowing it had been Elsa's choice. I looked around. His eager eyes were on me almost imploring. I waited.

'It's this murder, you see,' he burst out. 'I wanted you to dig into it. An old case. Twelve years old and more.'

I poured the water placidly; my nerves jumped. 'Milk?'

'Yes,' he said. 'You may have heard of it. They hanged him. All you'd have to do is dig out all the facts. It wouldn't take you long.'

It wouldn't take me any time at all. 'What's your name, son?'

'It's Hutchinson. Paul Hutchinson.'

For one moment I'd wondered if he was going to say Gaines. There'd been a daughter, but I hadn't heard of a son. 'Nobody can help the poor devil if he was hanged.' There was still a chance it was another case. 'What was his name?'

'A chap called Neville Gaines. Here, I bet you can even remember him. You're old enough.'

I'm thirty-three. 'I think I remember it.' I sipped tea. 'There's nothing there. He did it sure enough.'

'Yes. Yes, I've no doubt he did.'

'Then why rake it up?'

'I thought ... there was a chance I'd got a new slant on it.' He had to fumble with his spoon. It was his first lie.

'And you want me to do the background work?' I waited for his nod. 'Then what?'

'There's a sort of idea I've got.'

Throw him out? Certainly. 'What's your interest in it?'

'Well—I'm kind of a writer.'

'What have you written?'

'Actually ... well ... this'll be the first.'

Give him time to finish his tea? Yes. No hurry.

'Ah, I see. One of those brilliant re-thinks of old cases. You'll throw doubts, I suppose, on various integrities, and finish up annoying a lot of people who'll sue the pants off you.'

I'd let him have it straight, get the air cleared. He blinked a bit and put on his glasses.

'I'd do my own research, but there're snags.'

So now we were coming to it. I went to look in the cupboard, and asked him if he'd like a biscuit.

'Lots of snags, son. To start with, you're treading on toes. The Gaines widow, for instance, wouldn't like it.'

'Oh, Myra's quite happy about it.'

Damn the lad, why'd he keep surprising me? 'Myra?' Myra Gaines would be getting on for twice his age, surely.

'I went to ask if she minded if I researched it.' His eyes moved. He took a biscuit. Another lie had crept in. He said warily: 'She was quite pleased ... really.'

'And what else?'

'There's a daughter.'

So there we were. He'd barged in there, all brash and naïve, claiming he wanted to re-think the case. Nothing personal, you understand. Only there'd been a daughter. Then things had abruptly gone wrong. Suddenly it became very personal indeed, and he'd realized it might not be such a good idea after all.

'Aged?' As though I didn't know.

'Oh—twenty-one.' He looked away. 'Her name's Karen. She's five-four or so, blonde, you know, kind of willowy, with those sort of far-off eyes that go all smoky when she laughs.'

'I get the picture.' I went and looked out of the window. A traffic warden was prowling. 'You'd expected to sit for hours with the family, digging out the little personal details that mean so much?'

'I suppose it would've been something like that.'

'But now you want somebody else to pop the questions?'

He lied again, more glibly because there was only my back to do it to. 'It would be better.'

I turned on him slowly. 'What did you mean—you'd got a new slant on it?'

He put on his glasses, took them off. 'Did I say that?'

'You know damn well you did. Earlier on you said you thought there was a chance you'd got a new slant on it. Have you got something, or is this just a matter of hoping?'

He should have left them on, then maybe the fear wouldn't have got through the smoked glass. 'Well naturally, one tries not to bring preconceived notions—'

I cut him off. 'Nobody dives unprepared into a thing like this. Nobody picks out an old and fusty murder case and plunges into it blindfold, hoping to bring in a new slant. Not even an experienced author. Not you, son. Certainly not you.'

There was half a biscuit pathetically in his left hand. He moved it towards his mouth, seeing it was open, then stopped. He waved it. 'One has to start somewhere.'

It wasn't me scaring him. He wasn't trembling and confused. Just persistent.

'It'd be eight quid a day,' I told him flatly. 'And expenses.

Could run out at quite a figure.'

'Then you'll do it?'

'No,' I shouted. 'Not until you tell me the lot.'

'I've told you all there is.'

'There's the bit about what's got you scared. You went into this like an innocent baby, for some reason you're keeping to yourself. Then you came up against a snag, so you decided to toss somebody else in, in case things got rough.'

He got to his feet. From somewhere he scavenged a little dignity. 'Then I'm sorry to have wasted your time.'

Stubborn, he was, I hated to see a frightened lad walk out of my door.

'I can't work unless the client levels with me.'

'I'm sorry you think I'm not.'

'Why pick on me, anyway?'

'Your name was mentioned.'

Fame, by heaven. I watched him reach the door. I knew I should not let him walk through and out of my life. He reminded me of that solitary magpie, alone in a cold expanse of snow.

'Who'd mention my name?'

'She married again, Myra Gaines. Her husband, it was, who told me. His name's Carter Finn.'

I prised the door handle out of his fist, locked my hand on his shoulder, and got him back to his chair.

'Have another biscuit. They won't be on expenses.'

He smiled. The fear went from the hard line of his mouth. Tiny wrinkles flickered at the corner of his eyes.

'That's very good of you, Mr Mallin.' He chose another biscuit. 'Is there any more tea?'

I looked. And there was.

CHAPTER TWO

What had seemed like a good idea at three o'clock had lost its attraction by six. The dinner jacket was pressed and I'd steamed out the musty smell. But I was no longer keen on taking Elsa along. Suddenly I was on a case.

From the middle of Birmingham it is an hour's run to Elsa's place in Shropshire. The Porsche squeezed it down to forty-five minutes. In a few more days I would no longer be doing the journey, and it would be my place in Shropshire, or pretty nearly. So I drove through the gates with some pride.

You come out on a gravel drive in front of the wide portico, and the house broods over you with a few hundred years of history behind the ivy. I liked the view of the rolling hills from the rear. I was going to be very happy living there, once I'd got used to being deprived of my little flat.

I was still wondering how to put it when I let myself in. Elsa, I was certain, would be half-way down the staircase in something Parisian, and I'd have no excuse for failing to take her along. But there was no sign of her.

'Elsa!' I shouted.

It was Doris's head that appeared over the rear hall balcony. Doris had been cook-housekeeper for unimagined years.

'Will you come up, Mr Mallin?'

I went up. They were in the west-front bedroom, the one that's furnished in grey and rose, the one that would be ours. It was chaos. Elsa's hair was flying and she had that rapt, wild look in her eyes of intense concentration. Elsa had always been emotional. I think she would be incapable of doing anything without extracting from it every last vestige of its impact. She looked at me, brushing the hair from her eyes with the back of her hand.

'Oh David—is it that time already?'

Her lips were dry. 'I may be a little early.'

'We're up to our eyes in it here . . . really?'

They were only preparing for a wedding. As far as I could see, all it needed was a couple of cases packing for our fortnight in Majorca. I looked round, but I couldn't see just what was causing the distress.

'Perhaps I ought to give you a hand,' I suggested.

'No,' she said. 'Oh no. You keep out of it. We've got enough to contend with as it is.'

I smiled at Doris, who flexed her lips a little. Maybe Doris didn't approve of Dave Mallin.

Still, it did look as though I'd got a let-out. I shrugged and slid out the cigarette case I use when I'm wearing the dress suit. 'I don't see where you're finding difficulty. At my end it's a reasonably sedate and controlled business.'

'It would be,' said Elsa. 'You can't imagine.'

Then she looked fiercely at Doris as much as to say: when's he going to get out from underfoot?

'So you don't really want me around?'

'Not if you've got anything else to do.'

I got out my casual smile and moved to the door. Elsa hadn't been too keen on the agency idea. She had inferred that I'd soon become bored with the silly idea and agree to live quietly as a country gentleman. It was just that I was anxious to insert some minor degree of independence into our relationship. I wasn't going to earn a fortune at it, but it'd keep me in pipe tobacco. There would be one small thing I wouldn't have to take from Elsa.

'I'm on a case,' I said, casually enough.

'David, you're not!' Somehow I'd expected some congratulation. All I got was her startled eyes and a voice of doom.

'It may not come to anything.'

'But now!'

Just because they were up to their eyes didn't mean I had to sit and wait—did it? 'Well ... yes, now actually.'

'David, how could you! It's so inconvenient.'

There was a lot I'd got to learn, obviously. I looked to Doris for guidance. Doris was nodding her grey head in solemn disapproval, pursing her lips like a little volcano with runnels of wrinkles all round it. What'd I done?

'I shan't let it affect us.'

'We're getting married on Friday.'

'I hadn't forgotten.' I tried a little smile, but it bounced off. 'Friday I'll leave free.'

'As though I haven't got enough to worry about!'

'Now Elsa love, if it's going to upset you ...'

'No.' She pounced in, shaking her head until her hair flew. 'No, no. If you must go on with these things, you must.'

'There's no must about it.'

'And afterwards we shall be in Majorca.'

'This case has waited for twelve years. It can wait another fortnight.'

She looked at me as though searching for the hidden insanity she'd previously missed, then she turned and flung herself at a suitcase on the bed, apparently unpacking in ten seconds what had taken an hour to place in there.

'And then we'll be back,' she cried, 'and it'll still be there. You'll go straight back to it. All through our honeymoon you'll be brooding over it. Blaming me for keeping

you away from it. I'd thought of us coming back here, and
... well, settling in. You know...'

I looked in agony at her back, her slim waist, the agitation in the movement of her head.

'Elsa—we've had all this over.'

'But to start a case now!'

'I'll pack it in,' I promised heavily.

She turned back to me. Her face was red, her lips full.
'Oh no. You're not going to have that to throw at me.'

Sometimes a little devil of anger stirs in Dave Mallin.
It flickers up and engulfs him for a second, then it's gone.
But while it's there it wreaks havoc.

'I'll bloody-well chuck it in,' I said furiously. Then I
turned and stalked out of there, and if she called after me
I didn't hear it because I made too much noise galloping
down the stairs.

It was not the sane behaviour of a man a few days from
his wedding. As I stabbed the Porsche's engine into life,
I was aware that I was going to regret it. All evening, until
I'd sorted it out, I'd be miserable and deflated. My hand
hovered over the ignition key. I looked up. If her face had
only appeared at the window I'd have cut the engine. But
the windows remained faceless. I spurted gravel all over
the daffodils in the border and the wheels were spinning
all down the drive, and I was out on the main road before
I remembered that the windows of that particular bedroom
were not visible from where I'd parked.

I had not been to The Beeches for over twelve years,
but I remembered very well where it was, only seventeen
miles from Elsa's, across country. But it was dark all the way
and all I saw of the countryside was a hedge in the outer
reaches of each headlamp beam. There was no hurry
because I'd come out of Elsa's earlier than I'd expected.
But all the same I hurried. I was hoping there would be

something to eat at The Beeches. There hadn't been anything digestible at Elsa's.

The blue and gold sign flashed into the lights. 'The
Beeches.' It could have been a hotel, a pub, a country
residence. It *had* been a country residence when Neville
Gaines was there—Myra Gaines's house. For the first time
I realized how close the situation was to my own with
Elsa. In both cases the properties belonged to the woman,
and in both cases the husband attempted to justify his
existence with a residual occupation. In Gaines's case it
had been painting, a gentle, placid occupation, which had
led him to extreme violence. My occupation wasn't gentle,
and I didn't expect it to be placid. I hoped it would not
lead to any sort of violence.

Twelve years before, I had driven Crowshaw up this
drive in an Austin Cambridge. I could remember it well,
well enough to realize that they had glossed it up a bit.
Through the trees lining the drive, which were now cut
back to remove the overpowering feeling of depression, I
could see that they had floodlights on the house. As I
swept round and clear of the trees the long terrace was in
full view. The floods were crouched back on the limits of
the terrace, bathing the noble front in orange light. It was
a long, squat building in red stone, with castellations and
turrets. There were columns ranged along the terrace, and
a row of high windows leading out on to it. The house
sparkled with light from every downstairs window. As I
swung round beneath the terrace on smooth tarmac, I
faintly heard music. There had not been this drive below
the terrace. The original drive had led directly ahead and
along the end of the house to the old stables, which, even
twelve years before, had been garages. But now they'd got
it laid out, in front of me a sign indicating that I should
drive all the way round to the parking lot. I did.

The greenhouses were gone. There was a spread of asphalt bordered by solid fencing, and two small search-lights on poles to give the impression that you left your car safely beneath their benign illumination. I backed in, and cut the engine. Then I got out and had a quiet look round, because I hadn't detected anybody watching me. Which was suspicious in itself at a Carter Finn establishment.

It was early, but there were about fifty cars there, mostly in the luxury class. I saw a 3 litre Rover automatic in grey that I thought might be Finn's. It was splendidly polished. Two cars away was tucked-in a red Mini with matt black patches. He'd beaten me to it.

Over to one side, leaning against the rear of the house, was the conservatory that Gaines had used as a studio. There was light in it.

I looked round and located the sign that said entrance, climbed half a dozen steps, and was inside the club.

What I had in mind, around that time, was to find Paul Hutchinson and tell him it was off. Then find a phone and call Elsa and discover whether that was still on. Because I was thinking of these things I smiled before I recognized the man walking towards me in a dress jacket that shone like a suit of armour. He touched his fingertips delicately together. Sandy eyebrows were raised in polite enquiry. This was Feeney Keston, last sent down for eight years for robbery with violence, now respectable and suave, but judging by his eyes still completely vicious.

'Good evening, sir,' he said. 'It's a very fine evening.' His eyes were flickering over me, searching for the elusive memory.

I said: 'David Mallin. Honorary member.'

Something related to shock stiffened his jaw. His cold eyes told me to wait. He disappeared inside a cubicle. In half a minute he was out. One of his ears was pink.

'Just go right in, Mr Mallin. On the house.'

I grinned at his pain; it must have cost him a lot to be so polite.

I pressed open a pair of plate glass doors and found myself at one end of what seemed like a wide corridor. Deep and placid red carpeting ran away from me invitingly. The light was subdued; it oozed rather than shone from the ceiling. Then I saw that it was not a corridor but a raised extension of the rooms to the right, which were three steps down and entered by way of a series of arches. Each archway had heavy plush curtains curtseying back to the pull of silken cords. There was the gentle sound of music.

I approached the first archway and discovered the ballroom. The tall windows on to the terrace faced me. Tables were spread around the outskirts and waiters moved discreetly amongst them, one of them coming up the steps towards me and smiling in polite apology as he brushed past, all the world as though he was as used to the tray in his fingers as a switch knife. There was a South American band on a dais at the end, at this early hour only toying with it.

I looked after the waiter, then followed him. A double curtain, then abruptly the corridor became a long bar running all the way along one side of the building. It glittered. The carpet became grey and the walls maroon and smoke. Light caught the multi-coloured fluid in a thousand bottles and sprayed it into the tinkling atmosphere. Low conversation and delicate laughter issued from the few people at the bar.

I bought myself a scotch, and saw nobody interesting. Only Troy. Right at the end, he was, wedged between the **extreme edge** of his stool and the corner of the bar, nursing three tall glasses and some private hatred that I hoped was not directed towards me. He was wearing a plum-coloured dress jacket with black lapels and a shirt with a lot of lace down the front. Very fancy. I hoped the gun wouldn't smear his frills with oil.

When the man brought my drink I asked him if I could get anything to eat around there. 'There's the Grill Room, sir.' I nodded. It was comforting.

I wandered along the bar with my drink and saw that the archways here opened on to the gaming room. Lower, shaded and frilled lights cast a romantic glow on the dis-creet hum and clatter of the wheels and the croupiers' *'rien ne vas plus'*, all very continental and impressive if one of them hadn't been Harry Klein, late of Tipton, and later of Winson Green prison.

'Quiet tonight.' I was standing next to Troy.

His eyes came into focus. 'Staying long, Mr Mallin?'

I'd been quite friendly about it. There was absolutely no cause for the distrust in his voice. 'I may be.'

'Then later, if there's time...' His mouth fought for it but didn't quite achieve a smile, '... a game of chess?' And he produced a pocket set from somewhere inside with his gun.

The poor devil was bored. I laughed, ran a finger down behind his lapel. 'Sorry, I don't play. Too deep for me.'

He was lost again, bereft. I left him to his sorrow, stepped down on to the gaming floor, and watched idly as some-body in a grubby old smoking jacket lost £100 on 23. I'm not a gaming man. I don't believe in luck. I never take chances, and sure enough I never win. I winked at Harry Klein. He almost choked over *'faites vos jeux'*. He called it fate.

But I had spotted a sign that said Grill Room.

Yet I was sure I'd appreciate much more fully the

delights that awaited me in there once I'd spoken to Paul and told him it was all off. At the far end of the gaming room there was a wall consisting almost entirely of glass, and beyond it an unearthly glow. The conservatory, that must be. As it was the only place, apart from the Grill, that I hadn't been, I looked. He was there all right.

They had extended it and lighted it discreetly so that it provided a restful retreat for persons such as Smoking Jacket who'd just flipped their last hundred down the drain. Greenery curled and looped, and a monstera scared me a little. The smell was hot and fleshy. Paul was kissing a girl where the fronds hid most of the action except the fact that he'd got his hand where a hand only gets after the kissing has been going on for some time—and was likely to continue. I withdrew.

She had been wearing a gold sheath dress and tights and a nice little watch.

I climbed five steps into the Grill. It was nearly empty. Tiny tables swam in a red glow so dim you could barely reach them. My steak and mushrooms were so expensive that I passed up the french fried, and when I clicked my lighter for a few breaths of tobacco until it came, the flash nearly blinded me in the gloom.

The steak was rare. I could tell that the moment my knife parted the surface. How it tasted I never found out.

A voice at my elbow said: 'Mrs Finn will see you now, sir. If you'll just follow me.'

He had a short jacket and a waist like a young girl, and he was bald. I looked in despair at my plate.

'Now?'

'If you don't mind.'

'And what if I do?'

Such an eventuality had never sullied his mind. Harsh reality tortured his face. 'Sir?'

Madam was waiting. To hell with food. I stood up. He relaxed, and his life slumped down into its placid groove.

There was a felt-lined door off the gaming room, and suddenly we were in the morose and echoing hall. Stairs mounted in triumph from the centre, the balustrades in hand-carved oak. They spread out at the top in both directions along a balcony. We went left. The carpeting pressed aside to let me through. There was no sound.

'In here, sir,' he said, and opened a door without, as far as I could see, touching it. I went in there.

It seemed I was in their private lounge.

For one thing, I had had no intention of seeing Myra Finn. For another, I wasn't keen on Myra Finn sending for me. After all, she wasn't even paying me. So all in all I was in no mood for pleasantries.

When she had been Myra Gaines I had seen her only a couple of times. She had then been getting on for thirty. Say forty to forty-two now. I was looking at a woman I'd have said was thirty-five, eager, alive—and welcoming.

She was slim, dressed very simply, but obviously with the intention—the habit—of circulating with the customers. Her dress was so simple they'd never be able to reproduce it, and she had a small diamond and turquoise brooch just over her left breast. There was a single gold band round her wrist, a wedding ring, no more jewellery than that. Her hair was worn high, with touches of grey in the chestnut. Maybe she'd put them in there for dignity's sake. She came towards me smiling, one slim hand extended, and her face was alive. There were fine planes between her jaw and her eyes, high cheekbones, and a straight nose. But it was her eyes that caught and held me, wide brown eyes with gold flecks and some hint of mischief, shared illicit joy ... I don't know. But she knew I was there. She knew and was glad I was there. I was made aware of it, and should have been warmed by the experience.

'I'm so glad you could find time to help me, Mr Mallin,' she said.

I liked the voice. It was deep and attractive. I wasn't keen on what it said, though, because there had been nothing in my brief about helping her.

'Can I get you a drink?' she asked.

I nearly said something about drinking on an empty stomach but managed to iron it down to a neutral smile. Let her play it her way, I thought.

She brought me a dry martini. I waited while she made something very elegant about lowering herself into one of the huge easy chairs, then I allowed its companion to accept me and conform to my eccentric shape. I was really living.

'Perhaps you'll explain in what way I can be of help,' I said very carefully.

'By finding an answer to this ridiculous business. It's really so worrying.'

Living as she did, in the very vortex of club life, she'd spent a lot of time looking at people over the edge of a glass. She did it to me quite expertly.

'If it's been worrying, I'm surprised you haven't done something before.' I looked at her over the edge of my glass, but I haven't got the eyes for it.

'Poor Neville,' she said. She paused, making a decision. 'Shall I tell you something, Mr Mallin?'

'I'm here to listen,' I assured her gravely.

'Then ... you wouldn't believe ... but in the past year or two I've hardly given a thought to Neville. Now, isn't that a terrible thing to say?'

Was it? I don't know. 'I don't think so,' I said. 'You went through a harrowing experience. Your husband was hanged.' Her eyes did not even flicker. 'It'd be nonsense to suggest you ought to spend the rest of your life brooding.'

'How very understanding you are.'

'It would have driven you insane.'

'It would. I'm sure it would.'

'So you'd hardly welcome its intrusion into your life at this stage,' I suggested.

She carefully put down her glass and followed the movement with her eyes. 'Welcome it?' She inclined her head sideways, considering it, being fair to the idea. 'One doesn't use such a word as welcome when it's a matter of duty— don't you think?' Then at last her eyes came back to me. 'I'd never done anything but assumed he was guilty, but of course if there's any ghost of a chance that fresh evidence could bring any new light to bear...' She made a little gesture of annoyance at her confusion.

'And is there?' Her eyes were blank. I prompted: 'Fresh evidence.'

'I'm sure I don't know.' Her eyes moved. 'It's all so vague. You must ask Paul.'

I'd ask Paul, right enough. I'd ask him what the hell he was playing at, tossing me in without all the facts.

'But he must have told you.'

'Oh ... something most confusing about the second gun.'

'What about the second gun?'

'Where it was found.'

I sipped my drink delicately. The dryness curled my tongue, and perhaps prevented me from blurting out something angry. What were they talking about? What could it possibly matter to Neville Gaines where the second gun was found? Paul Hutchinson had dug out a widow who had let the whole thing drift into the blissful past, and now we'd got a widow who felt she ought to make a gesture and launch a campaign. The 'should Neville Gaines have hanged' brigade. With Dave Mallin at the head, probing inconsequential little details that weren't going to do anything but raise a snarl here and there. But I supposed it'd be useful to have Dave Mallin around to be snarled at.

'So he came to you,' I said. 'This Paul Hutchinson. He came with some nonsense about where the second gun was found, and all of a sudden you're running round in little circles wondering whether the trial was fair...'

'One has to do something.'

Did one? 'You could leave it alone.'

She got up then. I'd been prodding at her in a tone as near to contempt as I dared to go, hoping for some reaction. She got up, and managed to translate the movement into a simple and unforced journey to the compact bar in the corner. She was a very controlled woman.

'Perhaps I've left it long enough.'

She had her back to me, probably prickling with anticipation of what I would say. So I said nothing. I waited while she brought the drinks. She was wearing a patient smile, but with her eyes blank. I took the glass.

'So what's new about the second gun?'

Where it had been found hadn't been the important point. That there'd been a second gun at all was what had mattered.

I'd managed to coax an edge into her voice. 'I don't know. You must see Paul. I'm so vague about this sort of thing.'

Vague? But she'd been in the middle of it. The damned murder had circulated round her; she had been the motivating force.

'What can you hope for?' I demanded. 'After this time any number of small points could arise. It'd be easy to say this should have been done, or that should've been

said. Then where would you be? Neville Gaines shot Andy
Paterson, and there's not any doubt about that. You can't
alter the fact that he was hanged. The best you could hope
for would be to show he might have been found not guilty.
How would that suit you? Would it make you rest any
sweeter at night, to think he might have got away with
it?'

Her eyes hadn't left me for one second, large, wide, surprised. When I stopped she glanced down at her glass.

'But I'd still need to know.'

'You don't need anything of the sort.'

'Still *have* to.' She glanced up angrily, then managed a
smile. 'So you'll look very carefully, please, Mr Mallin.'

'And report to you?'

'You must report to your client, of course.'

And how was that going to help her? It wouldn't, as
far as I could see. It seemed to be time I left.

'I can let myself out,' I told her.

Her eyes agreed, so I did. He was hovering in the corridor, baldy, making sure I didn't leave with any of the
silver.

They were no longer in the conservatory. The exercise
they had been conducting would have had to be concluded,
one way or the other, long before. I thought maybe I'd
ring Elsa there and then, and have done with it, but I
decided to give him one more chance. They were in the
ballroom, dancing to a sleazy tango. Neither of them was
smiling. Paul looked a little flushed. Oh well—no time to
lose. I went in and tapped him on the shoulder.

It wasn't what I meant. He flashed me a look almost of
gratitude, and handed her over. The tango is not one of
my greater accomplishments.

She was, as Paul had said, willowy. She wore her blonde
hair short, and her eyes were definitely smoky, somewhere

between grey and blue, and deep. She had not been smiling at Paul, but she found one for me.

'You're Karen,' I said, because I'm very quick.

'And you're David.'

So there we were, my hand stuck in the cleavage at her back, and she moving beautifully against it.

'He's told you, then?' I asked. It was getting around.

'Silly boy.' I was not sure which she meant.

'I think there's been some sort of misunderstanding,' I said.

'You're a private eye, aren't you?'

'I need to have something to look at.'

She smiled again. There were signals in the smoke. 'But as long as you're paid...'

She was very close. Her hair smelt of heaven. 'I keep making the necessary movements,' I agreed.

'To and from the bank?'

I don't know what it was about me; I seemed to be attracting aggression from the most unexpected quarters.

'If I get paid. So far I'm doing nothing but make polite noises.'

She didn't like that. There was a fractional tightening of the hand on my shoulder. 'You went out of step.'

'I'm always out of step.'

'Then you should try harder.'

'I need the practice, that's what it is.'

The moment had passed; we'd touched swords. She withdrew, smiling, her little nose quivering. 'You must come again. I'll give you lessons.'

'Free membership,' I said. 'Now free lessons.'

'Everybody wants you to be happy.'

'Everybody,' I agreed.

Except the band, which switched to a bosa nova that left me completely wrong-footed. So I took her back to Paul, who was seated at a corner table looking morose and impatient.

Carter Finn was sitting with him. He stood as we approached. He never even glanced at Karen.

'Want a word with you,' he said.

The tables were nearly all occupied by now, and I saw that Myra was circulating dutifully. She seemed to know everybody. Her personality was crackling clear across the floor. As I watched, a man at one of the tables touched her arm. She turned to him with a brilliant smile, and her laughter beat through the bosa and gave something new to the nova.

'In my office,' went on Finn, seeing my eyes were occupied. His voice had gone very thin. I turned and saw Karen flash a glance at him. No smoke now—fire rather.

His office was just beyond the phone cubicle I was aching to get to. We were alone. There was a desk, and a combination safe in the wall making no attempt to look like anything else. I slumped into the one easy chair. Finn went to his desk, but only to get a cigar. He clipped it and lit it and looked down at me.

'You've seen her? What do you think?' I said nothing. After a moment his teeth showed. 'You didn't think anything?'

'I may report to my client.'

He rolled the cigar between his fingers. There hadn't been any suggestion that I should try one.

'Mallin, I want you to go carefully,' he said at last. 'She's my wife. She's not Myra Gaines any more. I don't want her upset. You understand?'

'It was Gaines who was upset.'

'Look it over,' he suggested. 'But make it easy.'

How many clients was I working for? 'I'm paid by the day, until I can tell my client the job's done.'

'Keep it short, and I'll see you don't lose by it.'

'I wasn't talking about me.'

He thought about it. His face was no longer affable.

'This where they sit?' I asked. 'All the mugs who can't pay their gambling debts and have to come and ask for time.'

'You asking for time?'

'And then you send for Troy, just for them to see?'

'You haven't got any time, Mallin. So don't try double-talking with me.'

I crossed my legs and reached for my cigarette case. 'Then send for Troy.'

His voice grated. 'I thought we understood each other.'

'Perhaps that's the trouble.'

I got up to use his table lighter, just to get the feel of it in case I needed something lethal in my hand. As I reached for it I felt him close behind me.

'Why not have a cigar?' he said softly.

I took a cigar. He had himself in control.

'I think we'd better start again,' he said. 'I wanted to keep everything friendly.'

But I'd had enough. 'You said it. Keep it short, you said. Maybe I will. I don't know. I'll follow my nose. At this particular moment, something smells.'

I stood in the bar for a moment, savouring the havana. There was no sign of Troy. So I went to the ballroom, where Myra was no longer circulating. Paul and Karen I could not see. I looked in the conservatory, in case they were retrieving something they regretted losing. They weren't. Nor were they losing anything else in the gaming room, though I did notice that Smoking Jacket had re-couped a little.

Just my luck. When I needed Paul, he had to go missing. And I certainly needed him just at that moment.

I went out into the parking lot. His Mini was no longer there. I cursed him and climbed into the Porsche, and wondered what were my chances of overtaking him.

What I should have done was drive straight back to Elsa's, and to hell with the lot of them. But as I say, I made the mistake of chasing after Paul Hutchinson.

CHAPTER THREE

He lived in Bridgnorth, he had said, and he'd mentioned a factory involved in electronics, where he was engaged on research. He didn't sound like a writer.

Because I didn't want to have to hunt out the address I drove fast in the hope of overtaking him. I had twenty-seven miles to do it in. The Porsche loves this sort of thing.

As I swung out on to the main road the first spatters of rain clattered against the windscreen. It was cold. I put the heater on. The visibility was poor, and the road was strange to me. To Paul it would be known. I began pushing things a bit, trying to make up on him.

There was a long, winding climb between near-vertical banks of glistening sandstone. The exhaust blatted back at me as I took it fast in third. Headlights ahead led me on. I was closing in. At the top I burst out into the open. Orange and blue streetlamps sparkled in the distance, uneasy through the lashings of rain. The headlights of two cars were plunging down the long and protracted hill in front of me. I rammed my foot hard down and the tachometer gave me an uneasy look.

We were diving down in sweeps and curves between rising fields and wooded slopes. For one second I would lose touch with them, then the lights would be there again. There was something disconcerting about the two cars— their lights were too close together. I caught blanketed glimpses of them as the rain curtain caught in the wind. Then I was close enough to be sure.

The Mini was being hounded by a larger car. You could tell by the erratic sweeps of the headlights, not entirely accounted for by the curves in the road, that the Mini was weaving frantically, beating off the other's approach.

I was on the limits of adhesion on corners, flicking into drifts. The wipers lashed away the streaming water angrily. The larger car was attempting to edge alongside, and the Mini was fighting it away. I could not see clearly. A large and dark car—but there could be no certainty. My tyres were screaming, the engine howl deafening me.

There was a half mile of open road, still sloping downwards, at the end of it a sweep under heavy trees. The cars touched, touched again. The Mini veered. It recovered, scraping the nearside bank, then plunged out of sight beneath the trees. I felt the tunnel of gloom pound back to engulf me.

Visibility was abruptly short. It was going to be tricky. I veered into the winding tunnel, touched the off-side bank with a steep drop beyond it, then howled round a corner in third—and rammed on the brakes.

Headlights were tumbling through the trees on my right.

The Porsche was still skidding when I fell out and ran back. Rain blinded me. The Mini had stopped plunging, and one light was still on, way below me through the shattered trees to where I could hear the roar of a small river. The bank was nearly vertical. Way ahead on the road was the distant whine of a high-powered engine disappearing into the distance.

Then everything was silent. I plunged down the bank with only the reflected light of that canted headlight to go on, slipping and sliding and reaching for tree trunks. It was on its side, one rear wheel still spinning. When I was twenty feet away the first flicker of flame trickled from

underneath. I let myself go, pitching forward so that in
the end the car stopped me. There was a heavy smell of
petrol. I scrabbled at the door I could reach. It was
jammed. The windscreen had crazed, but there was no hole
in it. I put my fist through as the flames grew round my
feet.

He was forward over the wheel, his head down and sideways on, twisted at an awkward angle. There was blood
flowing from his mouth and his eyes were open, turned up,
blind. I think he was dead. I tell myself he was dead.

There was nothing I could do. Heat lapped around me.
I pounded at the door, but it would not budge. Then
there was a surge of igniting fuel and the heat flung me
back, rolling. I twisted round, sliding on my side with the
left sleeve of my jacket smouldering. I came to a halt and
dragged myself around. Slowly I crawled up past the car.
The flames were licking sparks from the pine needles
above. I went on past, awkwardly and painfully back to the
road, crawling.

The Porsche was side-on in the middle of the road. headlights still blaring. Nobody had come along. I got in and
drove on. There was a phone box just over the bridge. I
dialled 999. The lot: police, ambulance, fire. Then I went
back and watched Paul Hutchinson's funeral pyre, gradually dying to a ball of concentrated heat. I dug out the roll
of nylon raincoat from my glove compartment, but the
suit was already ruined. My cigarette case had fallen out,
somewhere down there.

The police car arrived first. They parked the white
Zodiac on the bank, and got out to have a look, pounding
their black leather fists into their palms.

'What happened?'

'I was behind,' I said. 'There was a big car seemed to be
trying to get past. I didn't see how it happened. The bend.'

I pointed back. 'When I got here he was down the bank.'

This one was very big and probably amiable, but he looked grim just at that time. 'You got to him?'

'I got to the car. No good.'

'Mmm!' They looked at each other. 'Was he dead?'

'Certainly unconscious.'

'Lucky.'

I agreed. Lucky. He gave me a cigarette.

The ambulance and fire engine arrived together, racing each other for it. They got foam going and rigged up some lights for when the flames would be out. Then they cooled it down with water. They forced the door open with a crowbar. What they dragged out was not recognisable. It was not a job I'd like.

I was down there while the lights were still on, looking for my cigarette case. I found it in the mud at the edge of the river, but I didn't pick it up until they doused the lights and I could reach inside the car on my way back and dig the keys from the ignition. They were still hot.

They took some details from me. Then the car went off with a howl of siren that hardly seemed necessary. The firecrew were neatly putting away their gear. I got in the Porsche and went on to Bridgnorth.

Paul had given me a few clues and the actual address. Hobs Terrace. Perched between High Town and Low Town, he'd said, up a steep run of steps cut out of the rock. He had mentioned a view of the river. I drove into town, carefully skirting the lower road, not making much fuss with the exhaust. I parked the car on the silent forecourt of a petrol station, and got out. Paul had said he had nowhere to park, so the steps obviously climbed directly from the road.

The rain had ceased. A few stars came out. I found a wicket gate opening on to a climb of steps leading off at an angle. Twenty steps up, there was a painted sign that said this was Hobs Terrace. I climbed on. The vertical sandstone surface nudged my left elbow; a tubular steel rail protected my right. At the top the steps opened out on to a bit of flat. There were two old houses, dug into the rock. I could see the river, with beyond it the orange street-lamps of the Kidderminster Road. This was the right place.

There was a little light. The two houses were numbered 37 and 38. I went round the side of number 38. There was a wooden outside staircase with a rickety rail. The places were old black and white buildings, pressed hard against the rock face behind. I got out Paul's keys.

I needn't have troubled. The door was a weak planked job with an old sneck latch. They'd fitted a new Yale, but they must have had difficulty setting it in the rotten woodwork. Somebody had leaned on the door, and it had opened.

I went in, but I knew it was too late.

Paul Hutchinson had two rooms, this sitting-room and a bedroom beyond. The window in here was tiny, with flowered curtains and a white earthenware sink beneath it. One tap—obviously no hot water. There was a table with a cover on it and two chairs, and an old easy chair in front of a fireplace that had an inset gas fire. The high mantel had a little skirt of the curtain material. There were genuine hand-hewn beams across the ceiling, low enough to cause me to duck.

The bedroom matched it, the window even smaller, the beams sloping to the roof-line. The bed was iron with brass knobs, but he had a candlewick spread on it. There was a chest of drawers that had a varnished surface, now worn down to bare wood. But there was no wardrobe.

I started in the bedroom and worked my way back to the butchered door. I was hoping for some notes, at least, of the lines his enquiries might have been taking. But I found nothing. In the living-room there was a kitchen cupboard against one wall, and in the left-hand drawer I found a loose-leaf binder with notes on electronic circuits. There was a whole run of radio manuals and text books in a low bookcase beside the fireplace.

Beneath the loose-leaf binder was a manilla envelope, eight inches by three. I picked it out by the edges only and squeezed it to open its mouth. A letter fell out. It was dated two months before and was from a firm of solicitors in Wolverhampton called Fiston and Greene. Mr Greene was writing. He said he enclosed a letter from Paul's father, which the coroner had now released. There was no enclosed letter, but there was a paper clip where it had been.

I put it all back, then put out the lights and went away. Paul had been a tidy lad. It was a pity his death had been so messy.

It was nearly one o'clock. My first case had lasted around nine hours, and I'd lost my client. Keep it short, Finn had said. He couldn't have had it much shorter than that. I decided to go back and tell him, watch the pleasure seep into him, and I wondered whether he would forget he had said I wouldn't lose by it.

The Beeches was still bouncing with activity. It was only one-forty when I drove in there again. I parked in the same spot. The 3 litre Rover wasn't where it'd been, but I wasn't sure it was Finn's anyway. I had a quiet look round, but there was no dark, large car that bore impact marks. It was time to go on in, I decided. No it wasn't. There were the old stables over the other side still to be investigated.

I limped round. My ankle was aching a little; nothing that mattered. I knew just where the stables were, because we'd parked in front of them the day I'd brought Crowshaw. This side of the house was where they had their front door. They had changed the stables into a row of eight garages with wooden doors. The first four were locked, so I left them alone. I tried the other four. The end one had something big crouching in the gloom. I closed the doors quietly behind me and searched for a light switch by touch. It turned out to be a length of cord with a knot in it. A naked bulb sprang into life.

It was the grey Rover. There was a dent in the front bumper—off-side—and a score along the bonnet. The doors were locked. I couldn't see any red Mini paint in the score. I turned to reach for the knot.

Troy had the door open a yard or so and was leaning on it with one hand level with his shoulder, preserving the plum-coloured jacket from contact. 'I wouldn't hang around here,' he said. 'It could be dangerous, Mr Mallin.'

It was the nearest his voice had approached to warmness, just a shimmer of water on the icy surface.

'I must have lost my way.'

He nodded. 'Some of the boys might have drifted round. They're very rough, the boys.'

'I was looking,' I said, 'for a large, dark car with scores along the sides.'

'Were you?' He stood back for me to leave. I heard a slight tinkle from the chain on his wrist. 'A pity you didn't find it.'

I agreed. 'You didn't give me time.'

'If I find one,' he promised, 'I'll let you know.'

'Thank you.'

'If you're around.'

He lit a small cigar and watched me walk away. I took it steady, a prickly feeling between my shoulders. But nothing happened to the back of my head, and I arrived safely at the club entrance.

Feeney Keston was still on duty. He looked shocked on

seeing me. His eyes were going up and down, taking me
in with horror. Then I realized. They had a tall mirror on
one wall, so I checked.

I had discarded the nylon raincoat. There was caked
mud all down the right side of my trousers and a scorched
hole in the left arm of my jacket. My tie was twisted and
drooping, the shirt soggy. I turned and grinned at him.

'I'd like to see Karen Gaines,' I said.

'Karen?' he asked. 'Karen Finn?'

'So you find her and bring her out here. Eh?'

He got the point, and went.

While he was away I tidied what I could. Then I lit a
cigarette to create an impression of lack of concern for my
appearance. She was three minutes.

She had changed her dress. Now it was something in
powder blue that ran in a very nice line over her hips.
The neckline was high, and she was carrying a tiny dress
handbag. Her eyes looked darker than I remembered them.

'Yes?' she said abruptly. 'What is it?'

'Where can we talk?'

She waved a hand impatiently. I suggested we went out
to the car. She was eyeing me with more tension than I
thought my appearance warranted. We walked together
down the steps.

When she saw how low the Porsche is she said use hers.
Her Rapier was only four cars away. I let her slide behind
the wheel and reach over to unlock the other door, then
I got in with her.

'It's Paul, isn't it?'

They have intuitions, as they call them, which are the
result of putting two and two together.

'There's been an accident.'

'He's hurt?'

'I'm sorry, Karen, but it's worse than that.'

She drew in her breath, clutched the little bag to her lap, and stared out over the wheel. 'He's dead?'

'Yes.' I looked at her. One of the floodlights glanced harshly through her side window and did unflattering things to the lines of her face. She hadn't got the fine planes of her mother's features. In the cross light her eyes looked wild.

'Tell me what happened.'

'He ran off the road. The visibility was very poor.'

'Oh Paul,' she whispered. 'Poor Paul.'

I offered her a cigarette. She took it automatically, and her eyes didn't focus on the lighter. Smoke bounced back at her from the windscreen. 'He was a good driver,' she said.

'Everybody makes mistakes. Some people take chances.'

'Yes. Yes, I suppose so.' She paused. 'He rather fancied himself, you know. Kind of a romantic, I suppose. He lived on dreams.' She turned to me then, quickly, her eyes bright and eager. 'He fancied himself as a rally driver. He always drove just a little bit beyond his abilities.' She sounded very mature, choosing her words so carefully.

'He fancied himself as a writer, too,' I said.

She looked squarely into the night ahead. 'Yes.'

'Which could also be dangerous, I suppose, depending on what he intended to write.'

'Oh that!' She delicately picked a morsel of tobacco from her tongue. 'Nobody took it seriously.'

'Then what did they take seriously?'

She seemed not to have heard. 'He was wildly enthusiastic.' She was already used to speaking of him in the past tense. 'Well, I mean ... you met him. You must have seen how he was.'

Yes, I'd met him. 'He was my client.'

'That silly business!'

'Which nobody took seriously?'

At about that time she became aware that I was cross-questioning her. I saw her shoulders stiffen. Then she relaxed, drew in smoke, then flashed me a look of entreaty. I smiled to show I'd received it, and duly noted it.

'Mr Mallin,' she said quietly, 'you'll need to remember I was nine when that terrible thing happened to my father. Other little girls have their fathers die. They get over it. Mine didn't die.' She drew in her breath and got the words out in one burst of passionate disgust. 'He was hanged.' She gave me ten seconds to consider it. 'Can you imagine what that would mean? I was Karen Gaines. My father was hanged. It followed me wherever I went. That's Karen Gaines. Her father was hanged. I could *feel* the stares, the ... the ... not contempt, but the kind of gloating horror. It was a morbid thrill for them.'

'I hadn't realized.'

'I've grown up with it, Mr Mallin. It followed me through school, college—mother sent me to the U.S.A. in the end—but it followed me there. Karen's father was hanged for murder.'

She turned on me with a burst of righteous anger. 'I was only nine! What had it got to do with me? Why should it haunt me?'

'I can see you wouldn't want the old mud stirred around.'

She dismissed that as too obvious and facile. 'It's not that. Not just the resurrecting of it all. I can face it now. You get a hard shell in the end. Yes, I could face it.'

'But you changed your name to Finn.'

She gave a short bark of angry, mirthless laughter. '*His* name! Yes. But not to run away from Karen Gaines. Oh no. It was just because he wanted it.'

So much affection for her? 'You must be very close?'

'He hates me.' She spat it out, turning her face to me, two heavy lines between her eyes.

I tried to look blank, while my mind was racing. Carter Finn was jealous of Karen, who was much too close to Myra for his liking. This name business had been just a tiny lever. It brought Karen within his own sphere; it inferred he shared her equally with Myra, dividing the influence. But it hadn't worked. Their mututal hatred kept them worlds apart.

'So it didn't help, changing your name?'

Dark fortress walls reared between us. She turned to me and the boiling oil was canted ready to pour. 'My father was hanged. Nothing can change that. Nothing can help.'

'Such as proving he was not guilty?'

She was startled. 'There was no suggestion of that. How could there possibly be?'

'Then of what?' I thought for a moment she was not going to answer. I added: 'Paul must have come to your mother with at least a promise.'

'I don't know what he said to mother,' she replied in a flat, defiant voice. I was losing her. The portcullis was down.

'But he perhaps gave you a hint?'

Then it tumbled out in a chaos of anger and distress. 'A hint! Yes, but you couldn't tie it down. Suggestions ... inferences. He was so proud of it, and ... secretive.' Both hands now gripped the wheel firmly, knuckles white with little peaks of reflected light on each knuckle. 'He thought he was doing me a favour! My God, a favour! What good was it to me if he could have proved my father should not have been found guilty?'

'Just that? No more than that?'

Her voice sounded weary, lacking in emotion. 'I'd live then with the knowledge that he could have gone free.

And I was expected to be pleased.' The small laugh was sickly.

'To some people it could matter.'

She looked at me blankly. 'What sort of people?'

'If he'd promised more—that he could prove your father was definitely innocent—you could claim his body from the yard in Pentonville and bury him in the family vault.'

Her breath hissed with shock from between her teeth.

'Get out of the car,' she said softly.

I had the door lever well over, ready to get out of there fast. 'But he never promised you that?'

She whirled out of the driver's side, slamming the door nearly through the bodywork. I'd really got to her. I watched her stalk away, her head high, the floodlights catching tossed highlights in the soft gold of her hair. As she penetrated the deeper shadows I saw the red arc of her cigarette, flung high and wide.

I got out of the car, not feeling too good.

Troy was standing by the Porsche. One hand was negligently in his trouser pocket, but there was nothing negligent in his bunched jaw muscles as he glanced after Karen.

'You're upsetting people, Mr Mallin.' And he stabbed out his cigar in a shower of sparks against my paintwork.

'There was only one way of telling her Paul's dead.'

Something moved behind the screen of his eyelashes. His mouth flexed. 'That's so, is it?'

I nodded. He reached into his pocket, produced a paper handkerchief, turned, meticulously polished the little patch on my paintwork, then screwed it up and threw it away.

'He wants to see you,' he said.

Finn wanted to see me. No argument. No discussion.

'Then take me round the other way.'

He did so. We walked in painful silence side by side. He was an inch or so taller than I am, but I thought I'd be a little heavier. I hoped I'd never need to take his gun from him. He moved with the controlled grace of a pacing tiger, softly beside me, and took me round to what had been the main entrance when it had been on ordinary residence. The door was open. We went into the hall that I'd already met.

Troy mounted the stairs lithely, three at a time, and did the same trick with the door. This time I was ready and spotted it. There was a button in the wall a foot from the doorway. The door swung open. I went in. It silently closed in Troy's face.

It was like a stage set. Karen was seated on the edge of the chair I had used. She had her legs crossed, one elbow on the higher knee and another cigarette going in the supported hand. She was looking across the room at nothing, and she did not turn when I entered. Myra was over by the magnificent fireplace, holding it up with one hand. She wasn't sparkling any more. Her eyes met mine at once. I was expected to tell her it wasn't true, perhaps. She looked startled, shocked. The turquoise and diamond brooch was no longer over her left breast, and there was a little tear in the material. Normally she'd rush to climb out of such a desecrated dress, so it couldn't have happened long before I arrived.

I looked at Finn. He was at the bar pouring himself a drink, and, I saw with approval, one for me. He was dapper in a sky-blue mohair suit. On the surface of the bar was the brooch. He had only just put it down. Karen would have arrived only a minute before me. It appeared that her entrance had interrupted something violent.

He came towards me with the drinks. His eyes were cold and deadly, his mouth hard. He had poured me a scotch and flipped in a dash of soda.

'More soda if you want it,' he said in a flat voice.

The air crackled with tension.

'Karen's just told us,' said Finn.

He didn't say they had only just heard, I noticed. But Myra was looking like a woman who *had* only just heard, and was appalled.

As she didn't speak, Finn said: 'What happened?'

I moved the hand with the glass in the general direction of Karen, who might have caught the movement but only lazily drew on her cigarette. 'She hasn't said?'

'There hasn't been time,' Myra put in quickly. 'Only that is was a car accident.'

'That was all I told her.'

Something passed between Carter Finn and Myra, a warning.

'There's more?' he asked.

'Where it happened,' I said helpfully. 'How it happened.'

I was showing the bull a flutter of the cape. His eyes took me in and assessed me. I couldn't have looked very dangerous. I certainly didn't feel dangerous.

'If there was an accident, it looks as though you've been in it.' He cocked his head in challenge. 'You haven't touched your drink.'

I was aware that Karen's attention had been attracted. Her eyes were on me. 'I think, perhaps, I'll have some more soda,' I said, 'after all,' and drew Karen to her feet at once. 'Let me.' Her hand was out for the glass, but I was casual about it, turning from her. 'No ... I'll get it,' I said, leaving her hand poised in the air, and it was Myra who was forced to ask, 'then you were involved in it?'

'Not my car.' I put the glass on the bar, leaving the remark hanging in the air. In the mirror behind the bottles on the shelf I saw the quick look of warning from one woman to the other. Finn's eyes were squarely and uncompromisingly on the small of my back. I reached out for the glass, diverted it fractionally, and picked up the brooch.

It was a plain setting in platinum and couldn't have been worth more than four thousand. On the back was a safety fastening, which was supposed to save you losing it if you bent to pick up a lousy quid note, and an inscription which read: 'Myra, my inspiration. Carl.' I put it down gently. Then I squirted more soda into my glass and turned back to them.

'Then why don't you say what you mean?' said Myra with pained indignation.

'I was close behind him,' I explained. 'Not close enough to save him—but close.'

Troy would have reported that I had been examining the Rover. I was playing a pretty game, tossing live coals from hand to hand, and hoping to keep them moving so fast I didn't get burned. Finn was no man you could bluff. He came straight out with it.

'How close?'

'Close enough to reach his car before the wheels stopped spinning.' I took a sip of my drink, the edge of the bar boring into my back. 'When I got to him the car was already on fire. Just starting.' Karen turned away. Myra's eyes were huge. 'The door was jammed. I couldn't get him out of the window. The whole thing just went up like a bomb.'

I lifted my left arm, letting them see the scorched sleeve. Myra shot a glance of entreaty at Finn, who responded, and said it for her. 'Was he alive?'

'I don't know. Unconscious, I think.'

Karen sat down suddenly. She spoke in a tiny voice. 'Carter will you get me a drink?'

He turned on her with anger, but what he saw in her

face restrained him. 'Of course.' He raised his eyebrows. 'Myra?'

I moved away to let him get on with it. Myra came towards me. 'You must have had an exhausting evening,' she said with sympathy. 'Don't you want to sit down?'

'It's all right, thank you.'

Finn spoke from the bar. 'Then you must have been mighty close, to get to him that quickly.'

'Chasing him,' I explained. 'Trying to catch him before he got home. I wasn't sure where to find his place.'

I allowed a little silence to build up, but nobody told me where to find it, and in the end Karen broke in.

'But you didn't quite catch him?'

She had been distressed in the car, ending up furious. I'd managed to shake her then. Now she was poised, her eyes more to her mother's distress than to her own. She accepted a drink from Finn, and he smiled as he handed it to her. He was taunting her about something, a private joke perhaps.

'I was about two hundred yards behind,' I said. 'I couldn't see what happened. Just ran out of road, I suppose.'

'Distressing for you,' murmured Myra.

'I was a bit upset.'

Karen stirred. 'I think you're as unfeeling as a rock.'

'Upset at losing a client,' I explained. They stared at me. I expounded on it. 'He was still my client, you see. Whatever other people might slide in about their personal little wishes and dislikes, Paul was the boss, because he was paying me. Or at least, would've been, if we'd got round to it. As it turned out, he owed me for a day's work and expenses. Come to think of it, it's his fault this suit's had it. He owes me for that, too. Of course I'm upset. It's time and money down the drain.'

I looked at them blandly. A small curl of disgust began to distort Karen's mouth, and she drank quickly. Myra put her hand to her mouth, bewildered. Finn smiled. Finn knew what I was saying. All right, he'd pick it up, play with it.

'It'll teach you to vet your clients in future.'

'How could I check he was going to die?'

'Ask for an advance.'

I grinned at him. 'You're very generous with advice.'

'You were chasing him?' said Karen suddenly, angrily.

'Wanted to catch him,' I tossed at her, not looking round.

She ignored the look Finn gave her. I'd got her caught up in it. 'Before he got home?' she insisted. 'Why was it so important to speak to him?'

'Maybe he'd got his cheque book on him,' I said. 'Who knows! The damned thing would be ashes now.'

Myra took a step forward. 'Karen!'

But Karen's eyes were bright. 'He's not answering.'

'If I'd caught him,' I said, 'I'd have told him I was throwing the case up. If he'd had his cheque book we could have finished it there and then.'

I'd built round to it, got her poised for it, and got absolutely nothing from it. Karen nodded. Lowered her head, rather. Myra looked in exasperation to Finn, who gave a short bark of cold laughter at my failure to strike sparks.

'If you'd caught him,' he said, 'he wouldn't have died.'

'Yes. Then perhaps I ought to take the blame.' I finished my drink. 'I'm having to take a lot for no return.'

Then, having thoroughly established the background to my integrity, I waited to see what would happen.

Without a word being said, they went into intense conference, and came up with a mututal disagreement. Myra and her husband looked at each other. She may have shaken her head; there was no mistaking the smile he gave her when he took her empty glass. It was the smile of a man who is hurting his wife, and enjoying it. Karen kept her eyes on her mother, entreating her, but Myra was afraid of something. Perhaps of Finn. At one moment Karen moved as though impelled to go to her mother, but a quick raising of the eyebrows held her. Finn saw it, and smiled.

'It's a pity you've got to drop it, Mallin,' he said.

'There's nothing in it for Mrs Finn.'

'Can you be sure?' she pleaded.

'Sleeping dogs, you know.'

'But surely, if Paul thought there was something...' She was the pitiful widow, now, suffering for her hanged husband.

'What d'you want me to say?' I demanded. 'There's nothing worth considering. Is that what you want to hear?'

'I'm not wanting,' she pleaded, overdoing it a bit.

Karen turned to her. 'Do be sensible, mother.'

Myra looked at me, asking for guidance. 'I feel that Neville might wish it.'

'Mother!' Karen cried.

'If there's any small avenue to be explored...'

'You're not thinking of me,' said Karen passionately. 'He was *my* father, and I've had enough of it. Enough!'

It was all most beautifully done. They had a perfect affinity, those two women. Myra could not decently abandon the project at the first chance. She must protest; she must be forced to give way. She gave me the slightest moue of protest, raising her eyebrows for me to appreciate her gentle pleading.

'But perhaps we could see that Mr Mallin isn't out of pocket.'

He had been waiting for it placidly. He could complete the thing with a shrug and a small cheque, and everybody would be happy. But Finn knew and I knew that I had seen the car, and whatever emotions the ladies might toss around, Finn knew it all came down to business. He was not sure he dared to buy me off—or in fact could afford it.

'I've already told him he wouldn't lose by it,' he said.

'Well then,' murmured Myra contentedly.

'So you could say I'm his client,' he went on. He smiled at me, like a smake uncoiling. 'Couldn't you?' And when I inclined my head he raised his glass to Myra. 'In which event I think he'd better go on with it for a while.'

Outrage forced Myra away from the fireplace. She could not have understood his reasons; to her it had to be personal. Karen reached up quickly and put her hand on her mother's arm.

'There's things we should know,' Finn said. 'Things that might be expensive to find out.'

I got the point. 'And tedious.'

But Myra was beyond control. 'Carter, what are you saying?'

The brooch stood between them. To Myra he was being perversely obstructive, in continuation of some dispute that had raged between them.

'Keep out of this,' he said sharply.

'Out of it? But it's mine! It's *my* affair!'

'Sit down,' he told her, 'and shut up.'

Karen was on her feet, her face flushed. 'How dare you!' She flung her arm back wildly. 'This is our business, Carter. You tell her to shut up—'

He made no attempt now to restrain himself. He turned on her with fury. 'Keep out of this.'

Then for a moment hatred out of all reason flared between them. She made an effort and found some reserve of dignity, and lowered herself back into her chair. She sneered in my direction. 'Give him some money and send him away.'

'If he gives me some money,' I said politely, 'I'll stay.'

Myra spoke distantly and with complete control. 'Carter, I don't think you appreciate how much you're interfering.'

'But I do, Myra. I happen to think Mr Mallin should go on with it. In fact, I insist on it.'

Then Myra turned away. She walked back to the bar, picked up the brooch, and held it against her dress.

'I'm not sure it looked its best,' she observed. 'I shall try it with another dress.' And with calm dignity she turned and headed towards the far door.

'Myra!' he snapped. If he'd used that tone on me I'd have flinched. She kept straight on. She opened the door. She went out.

'Carter,' said Karen happily, 'you're a fool.'

The scene had cost him a lot—I saw it in his face. But he didn't intend to lose on the investment. He looked at me. There was bleak intention in his eyes.

'But we understand each other?'

I understood very well indeed. Played right, it could make me a small fortune.

'I'm beginning to,' I assured him.

CHAPTER FOUR

I was still understanding him right out into the corridor. Troy wasn't there. By the time I reached the balcony it occurred to me that possibly Finn was being quite subtle. He had married this thing, and it wasn't the same as a clean gang killing. It would have been too damned personal for him, the Gaines thing, and he'd feel uneasy until it was completely buried, way down deep. Look how he'd had Karen adopt his name. Maybe that had been more than the dissolution of the surname Gaines. So now, maybe, he was searching for something more positive to erase the name from the records.

Troy was standing in the hall, his back to me, his feet slightly spread. I made no sound, I thought. I went in quietly and got a foot on the hall parquet before I discovered what he was doing.

He was practising his left-handed draw. With one clean movement he whirled on the ball of his left foot, his right foot spread behind. He was perfectly poised. The muzzle of the thirty-eight was steady on a point between my eyes.

'Bang, bang, bang,' he said.

'You'll do somebody some harm with that,' I told him.

Then he laughed, a grating sound, and tossed the gun at me. I caught it in front of my face. It was plastic.

I smiled admiringly, and wondered where he kept his real one. Probably in his belt, just over his left hip. His jacket lapels were cut low, bowed gracefully over his chest, so that he could get in fast with his right hand. The jacket was a beautiful piece of tailoring.

'You're good,' I said, and gave him back his toy.

We walked together back to my car, and seeing he was in a good mood I asked him about the brooch. 'Who's Carl?'

I felt him shrug in the darkness. 'Comes here regular. Sits there in a rotten old smoking jacket, throwing the cash around. Something big in Brummagem.'

He knew what I was reaching for. I prompted him.

'Been giving Myra presents, has he?'

'Only one. He could afford it.'

We were out in front, looking in on the action through the tall windows. There was still plenty going on.

'Won it?' I guessed.

'One big bang.' Then he unbent. He'd got a story, and people love telling stories. And Troy was bored.

It'd been a month before. Myra was doing her circulating act, and was in the gaming room. She was standing at Carl's shoulder, lending decoration to the roulette table, one hand on his arm. 'Seventeen, darling,' she said, because Carl hadn't been having the luck, so Carl put a hundred on seventeen, and Myra clapped her hands when it came up. Carl was reaching out to rake in the winnings when she said leave it on darling. She hadn't meant the hundred, she'd meant the lot. That meant a delay while they fetched Finn, because they had a hundred maximum stake rule. Carl wanted to put a clear thousand on seventeen. You could just see it, Finn using his shiny smile, and Myra challenging him from Carl's shoulder. He'd agreed. The thousand went on seventeen. Or course, the odds on seventeen coming up again are just the same as for any other number, but they're a superstitious lot, the gaming crowd. Everybody went tense. And seventeen came up.

'He lost a lot later in the evening,' said Troy, 'but he carried home quite a wad. Nineteen thousand.'

So he'd bought Myra a diamond and turquoise brooch
—with Finn's money. And Finn was obviously delighted!

Troy leaned on the car while I got in. He was very close
to being friendly—something he'd have to watch.

'The boss don't like anybody paying too much attention to Myra,' he said, as though it was a warning.

I drove away. Nobody had to worry. Myra wasn't my
type.

I got in around three. I hadn't eaten for about twelve
hours, and there wasn't much in the cupboard, but I put
it all together in a pan and fried it up, and had it with a
can of beer. Then I fell into bed.

At eleven in the morning I went down to the hall and
phoned Elsa. I hadn't shaved, but I didn't reckon she'd
notice.

'David, where have you *been*?'

'I went to a club. Remember?'

'I've been trying to reach you.'

Had she? There weren't any messages. 'I'm sorry. Something cropped up, has it?'

'How can you be so casual? How *can* you, David?'

I didn't know how I managed it. So I said nothing.

'Have you got it arranged with your brother?'

Ted was going to be best man. I said it was fixed.

'Have you phoned to check?'

'Elsa, he isn't coming down till Thursday.'

'Still—you ought to check. And the taxis...'

I'd seen to the taxis.

There was no mention of my ridiculous bout of temper.
I needn't have tried three times to force myself to the
phone.

'Shall you be over?' she asked.

I hadn't planned anything yet. 'I'll be over.'

'When? I'll need to know.'

Lord—when? There were other things. 'Say about four? Hell I'd never fit-in the solicitor now.

'Don't be late,' she said. 'Love.'

I told a dead phone I loved it, because she'd hung up. Then I called the Shropshire County Police and asked for Crowshaw. What I hadn't expected was that he'd retired. 'Where can I find him?' They asked me to wait. They came back.

He lived, they said, at West Lees Farm.

I was half-way back up the stairs before it hit me. West Lees Farm had been Andy Paterson's place, and it was there that Neville Gaines had shot him to death.

Well at least I knew where to find it.

I cleaned up and had a bit of lunch across the way. It was raining again, so I threw my rubber boots into the car in case the farm hadn't improved since I saw it last.

West Lees Farm is only eight miles from The Beeches. It lies in the arms of the Brown Clees, an ugly old place high above the road, visible a mile away but not easy to locate from the road because a rise in the ground hides it from its gateway. Nothing was changed. I remembered the gate set back from the road in the thorn hedge. There was a pull-off, where you could park while you unfastened the gate. I parked and unfastened it. Just here Neville Gaines had left his Morris Minor. We had found an oil drip from his leaking differential. We had also found oil in the glove compartment of his car, where one of the thirty-eight Colt automatics had lain during the run over.

The drive was straight, a broken tarmac road, flat at first across fields that would probably flood, then rising past the bailiff's cottage to the farmhouse, peeling white and starkly bleak. It was set back behind a row of lurching trees as a windbreak. The drive swung round, then through to the yard.

I had seen no sign of stock. The bare, red mud was still there, but controlled. I decided I'd manage in shoes. There was a Land Rover parked over against the house, and something else darkly tucked into what had been a barn. I knew my way. Over in the corner was a wicket gate. Before I reached it, Crowshaw appeared along the side of the house.

Twelve years had done terrible things to Crowshaw. When I'd known him he'd have been around fifty, a stern and greying man with a small moustache. But now his shoulders were bent and he'd lost a lot of weight. The moustache had gone, leaving a rather deep upper lip, and his lower lip had sunk in. He was gaunt, and now his hair was completely white. A pair of grey slacks hung emptily about his legs and he had on a green roll-top sweater. Only his eyes were the same, greeny-brown, observant, and direct.

'My name's Mallin, sir,' I said. 'You probably don't remember me...'

'Of course I do.' Heavy veins lined his hand. 'You used to drive for me.'

'I drove you up here, that day.'

'I remember.'

He led the way round the side. There had been work done on the landscaping that Andy Paterson had commenced. A terrace and then ordered lawns fell to the orchard, beyond which the Clees rose in sombre greys and greens, the pines like a fine saw-edge against the sky. Paterson had been one of those bluff types that slap you on the shoulder and make bleating noises when they laugh. But he'd been a big, handsome man, and was a generous host. The impression we'd obtained was of a man scrabbling at the edges of county society, with some pretensions of sharpening up the place, possibly to the point of hunting parties. In the meantime he'd had a herd of Jerseys, and the closest he'd got to the hunt was the set of prints on the walls of his living-room.

When we got inside I saw that Crowshaw had kept the prints. But not the Jerseys, apparently.

'Grain,' he said, when I asked him. 'I never did fancy a stock farm.'

It couldn't have been an antipathy for animals. He had an Irish Setter and a Golden Retriever absorbing the heat from the fire. They raised their heads and flopped their tails, and then went right on with it.

The room was the focal-point of the house. It was long and low, with black and gnarled beams disappearing in vanishing perspective along the length, giving an impression of immensity. The fireplace was huge, built from sandstone blocks, the old andirons still there. He had a log fire going in it. Beside the fireplace was the long, leaded window which gave such a magnificent view over the hills, with beneath it a wooden settle, bearing a few scattered magazines. On the opposite wall a Welsh dresser carried a display of Crown Derby. There seemed to be no modern comforts such as radio and television. But he had a lot of books and some very large and comfortable chairs. The one he steered me into was a rocker.

Even when I'd known him before, Crowshaw had been a widower. I'd have thought he'd be lonely, in that great empty house all by himself.

'What brings you here?' he asked pleasantly enough, but his eyes were sharp.

I told him I was no longer in the force. He asked me what I was doing, and laughed shortly at that. 'But there's nothing for a private detective here,' he said.

'It was you I wanted to see, not the farm.' He nodded. I went on: 'I was rather surprised to find the two together.'

'Not really surprising,' he said, leaning forward and putting the tips of his fingers together. 'That case—the Paterson murder—brought me into contact with the place, and I came to grow fond of it.'

His eyes surveyed me calmly. I smiled while my mind scrabbled for it. What had there been to attract him? It had been a cold, rain-slashing November, visibility down to half a mile and no view of the valley. And Crowshaw, though a county policeman, was a city type. But the county police don't get many murders, and Crowshaw had reached Chief Inspector without handling one—until Andy Paterson died. So perhaps he'd wanted to live on the scene of his triumph.

'Yes, I can see that.'

'It came up for auction when they'd settled the estate. So I bid for it, and got it.'

So he'd owned it long before he'd retired. How could he have worked the farm and run his job . . .

'Drover's still with me,' he said.

I was disconcerted at the way he'd read my mind. But of course. Drover, who had been Paterson's bailiff—most likely bailiff for Paterson's father—had been there.

'But you're not interested in this,' he said, smiling.

I was, intensely. 'Not really,' I agreed. 'But it's the Paterson business.'

'Now? After all this time?'

'They raise their heads.'

'Best left alone, I'd have thought.'

'I've been asked to look it over again.'

He made an impatient sound and got up to poke at a log with his toe. 'What's there to look at?'

'Mrs Gaines,' I said, 'is now remarried to a man called Finn. She's had stirrings of something or other. You know how it is, they remarry, and the husband finds it's a weight he'd rather do without.'

'Prove that Gaines didn't do it? Nonsense.'

'Completely,' I agreed. 'But I get paid for it.'

There was unshadowed contempt in the curve of his wide mouth. 'You get paid for coming and talking to me?'

'I'm not told how to go about it.'

'There's the trial transcripts, the reports—'

'I've got all that. But you're forgetting, sir, I was a very young constable then, and I never got in behind the scenes. I thought ... well, if you gave me a background of how you saw it all, the things nobody can find out from all the reports in the world...' I shrugged. 'I could at least show her something for my time.'

He looked at me for a long time, wondering whether to encourage me in my stupidity. Then at last he said:

'There'll be a lot to tell. I'll go and make some tea. A sandwich, perhaps?'

I agreed, a sandwich. He turned and went out, and I watched him all the way. There seemed to be a lift to his shoulders that was new. But perhaps he was only exhibiting defiance. A man like Crowshaw could be expected to resent anybody questioning the conduct of his greatest case. Was he displaying magnanimity in agreeing to discuss it with me?

While he was away I got up and walked round the room, just from habit. I went and stared out of the wide window. A half mile away a tractor was crawling like a beetle across the green of a sloping field, scattering something. I picked up a magazine. *The Field*. It fell open to an article about the re-appearance of a rare swallow in Perthshire. In the margin was a doodle. It made nonsense until I turned it sideways and saw it consisted of those jagged and blocked symbols they use in radio. I was looking at an electronic circuit.

I went and sat down again. The setter came and put

his nose on my knee. I recalled that I'd left the magazine lying open, with the circuit visible, but before I could dislodge the brown nose Crowshaw came back with a tray.

'You'll need to excuse my memory,' he said. 'These things lie dormant, undisturbed, and you lose a few details.'

So I excused his memory, which was as unreliable as a computer, while we drank tea and ate tomato sandwiches.

In the end I was glad I had come.

CHAPTER FIVE

Crowshaw didn't need to remind me that the call had come through at about ten on that Tuesday morning. He sent a sergeant off—it was Freer, a cynical bastard if I've ever seen one—with a squad of men, and we followed an hour later in the Cambridge.

It had stopped raining at last, but the place was drenched, sodden. There were about a dozen vehicles parked down the drive, because the man from the local station was good, and he'd stopped anybody from driving up to the yard. The medical examiner had pronounced Andy Paterson well and truly dead.

Freer met us, grimacing. There had been an enigmatic footnote to the original report: better bring rubber boots. You could see what it meant. I've never seen such mud.

'He's over here, sir,' said Freer.

There was a stocky, intelligent-looking man at his shoulder, a strong man in his fifties. Freer said: 'This chap found him. Drover's his name. He's the bailiff.'

We went to have a look, plodding through the mud.

'Is it always like this?' said Crowshaw.

Drover had a pronounced Shropshire burr in his voice. 'Mr Paterson hardly ever came this side of the house.' He inferred that Paterson didn't care how it was.

But he'd come there on Monday night. The yard was an irregular expanse, bounded at one end by the rear of the house. It had four entrances leading from it, and it was blocked in with buildings, some quite decrepit; a hayloft nearly full of squared bales, two barns with scattered machinery inside, a pig-sty in the corner—but no pigs—and an old cow byre that was no longer used, but hadn't been cleaned out since it was. The byre had a large sliding door, which was stuck a matter of four feet open.

Drover had been in Kidderminster all day Monday, at a cattle show. At the time of the estimated death, which turned out to be eleven to twelve at night, he had been over at a friend's house there, discussing sileage and yields and things. He had driven up to the farm early on Tuesday, and saw Paterson as soon as he drew into the yard. He was lying half in and half out of the byre doorway, looking like a hunched pile of old clothes, with the mud rather redder than usual all round him. Drover took a quick look, then backed out his pick-up and drove down to his cottage to phone the police, and returned to stand guard, I suppose having fine regard for footprints in his glorious mud. As it happened, his precautions were of little help, because in the night a couple of Jerseys had pushed through a broken hedge and tramped heavily round Paterson's body, no doubt probing him with their wet and curious snouts.

Paterson was full of bullet holes. There turned out to be six in his body, the last two being lethal. There was blood soaked into the rotted lower edge of the door frame.

We looked around, six of us that first day, watching where our feet went. There gradually emerged a picture of what must have happened in that sodden darkness. There were drag marks, spent bullets in woodwork, and empty shell cases lying naked and gleaming on the mud surface, over a wide area. A pattern began to form. We discovered fractured twigs and a trail of blood from a shattered leg, the frantic finger marks of Paterson wrenching himself through the mud—and the pattern consolidated.

Andy Paterson had been hunted to death.

He had brought himself eventually to the cow byre, no doubt hoping to drag himself inside and survive in its obscurity. There the murderer had stood and emptied his gun into the huddled figure, while the cows lowed and red mud oozed round his ankles.

The gun we found at once, tossed away in the yard as the murderer flew blind into the night. The shell cases were also easy. Two were beside the byre entrance, five more scattered near the trail Paterson had made as he crouched and scuttled. That was pretty good, considering the territory; seven shell cases for a seven-shot gun.

But Crowshaw was looking bleak at that time. We were doing too well, and too quickly.

By the time I drove Crowshaw home that night, Neville Gaines had been arrested. There hadn't been much trouble about it. The car had been seen, parked by the gate. Drover said that such a car was owned by Gaines, and when we went to The Beeches he'd done nothing to cover up. There was a suit and shoes plastered with red mud, and he admitted the whole thing. He made a statement. He had gone up there with a gun with the intention of shooting Andy Paterson, and in the end he'd done it, finishing by standing over him at the cow byre and emptying the gun into him. His prints were on the gun we'd found, in spite of the mud.

A couple of days later things started to go severely wrong. Seven empty shell cases had been bad enough, because it was a bit too good to be true. But now the experts got into their stride and started doing things with spent bullets, and bullets in the body, and whatnot. They sent Crowshaw a report, which of course I never saw, which showed that four bullets had lodged in the body, one had gone straight through, and three spent ones had not gone through flesh at all. That was eight, not counting a sixth hole in Paterson, for which no bullet was ever found. Nine in all.

Crowshaw says he'll always remember that report landing on his desk. They were in his office, he and Freer. 'They must be crazy,' he said, wanting desperately to reject it.

Freer had a touching faith in science. He just smiled, and suggested they had another go at Gaines.

'But it's only a seven-shot gun,' Crowshaw protested.

They had Gaines in a cell below, and they had already seen him a number of times. But Gaines was already emerging as a vague and unworldly type of person, and anyway he was in a state of delayed shock.

Neville Gaines was a massive man with great shoulders and a head of long and shaggy hair. I was there at the arrest, and I remember most his eyes, soft, dreamy and emotional. He had hard and strong hands, but they moved with persuasive and not aggressive gestures. There was nothing aggressive in him that I saw, and when they got to him that day he was weary and defeated—resigned. He had done what he had to from an intense inner urge, and it had drained him. Crowshaw told me that he had to go very carefully with Gaines, and I've tried to reconstruct the scene as he remembered it.

'We would like to know,' said Crowshaw, 'how many spare cartridges you took with you.'

Gaines took a long time to answer, dredging down into his mind. 'Spare ... no, there weren't any spares.'

'How many shots did you fire into him?'

'All of them.' He spoke dully, and there were twitches at the corner of one eye, one for each impact as he pulled the trigger. But going on and on. 'I did what the man said. I pulled the trigger. I just went on pulling it.'

Crowshaw tried again. 'How many times?'

Startled eyes came up. 'On and on. Oh ... a dozen times. Twenty. I don't know.'

'Twenty? There were only seven in it.'

'It was a long time I stood over him. At the end. Yes ... I remember, a long time—and I kept doing it. But there wasn't anything happening. Not then. The thing wouldn't do anything at all. I threw it away and ran off.'

To Crowshaw it sounded so real and true.

'But you managed to re-load it?'

But they'd gone over all that before, when Crowshaw had been probing Gaines's familiarity with guns. Gaines seemed not to remember. 'I just bought the thing from this man called Lovejoy, and he'd said it would fire seven.'

'Which seemed to you enough?'

'Enough?' Crowshaw watched as the brain struggled with the memory. 'Enough for what? I don't know.' Gaines shook his head and his wild hair flew. 'I didn't think about that. The thing ... that gun itself, was enough. Just the buying of it. Just having it. Yes, yes I suppose you could say it was enough.'

Crowshaw left it at that. He was worried because this was a loose end in his case. The prosecution could prove— would undoubtedly have to prove—that at least nine shots were fired, and the defence could catch them in their own net by showing that Gaines had had only seven to fire. There'd be a complex argument about whether Gaines could have re-loaded. It wouldn't help Gaines, not with the strength of the rest of it against him. But it would cast doubts. And with the question unresolved Crowshaw dared not take his case to the Public Prosecutor's office. What had seemed to be a routine case was turning out to be very tricky indeed.

'The devil of it is,' said Crowshaw to the sergeant, 'that there could well have been more than nine. You can't tell me that an amateur like him would manage to get six shots into his man—in the dark—out of nine.'

'I'm just thinking he maybe had two guns.'

And as Crowshaw was aware that none of the bullets had distinctive markings, it seemed a good idea to proceed on those lines.

'Let's have Lovejoy in again,' he decided.

Gaines had been quite open about Lovejoy's name and address, which had placed Lovejoy in an awkward position, because he was a well-known figure to the Birmingham City Police. Being a potential Crown witness he was protected from prosecution on this, at least, of his many faults. He was expected to reveal enough, though, but he was aware that revealing too much would undermine his reputation in the underworld. His attempts to steer a neutral course were already playing on his nerves, and when they got him in again he twitched noticeably in the chair in front of the desk.

'Now tell me again,' Crowshaw invited. 'How many guns did you sell to Neville Gaines?'

'Only one, Mr Crowshaw.'

'I've got reason to believe it was two.'

'Now why should I tell a lie?'

'Maybe you think you've gone far enough, admitting to one.'

'I didn't have—'

'Any alternative? Precisely. But if he'd asked for two ... what then?'

'He only wanted one.'

'So I take it you'd got more? If he'd asked.'

Lovejoy looked pained. 'I'm not saying that.'

'But you are.' Crowshaw smiled. Sometimes he enjoyed himself. 'Would there have been another, if he'd asked for it?'

'No.' Lovejoy shrugged. 'Not another thirty-eight.'

Crowshaw seized on the inference. 'You mean,' he said softly, 'he *asked* for a thirty-eight? In those words.'

'Yes.'

It contradicted all that Crowshaw had learned about Gaines. That he should have gone in search of a gun at all was difficult enough to accept; that he should have been so specific seemed completely out of character.

'*One* thirty-eight?'

'He said—could I sell him a thirty-eight automatic.'

'Which you could? And did.'

Lovejoy made a shambling shrug. 'I told you, Mr Crowshaw, it so happened I could put my hands on ...'

Shortly after that they threw him out.

Crowshaw wanted time to think ... and he hadn't got it. A report had to go in every day to the Chief Supt., and what was he going to put in that day's effort? No progress.

Freer moved from the window. 'I think you scared him.'

'You heard what he said. Gaines specified a thirty-eight.'

'So what? Maybe he'd been reading some thriller or other, and Gaines thought there was something magic in the words.'

But Crowshaw was unconvinced. Instinct told him there was something he should understand, and logic told him that there were two guns and be damned to explanations. He was not sure which line to take.

'What did you make of Mrs Gaines?' he asked, wondering if it had been a good idea to trust that interview to Freer.

'I think she tried to seduce me.'

And Crowshaw tried to laugh it off. 'On the sofa?'

'With her eyes.'

Freer was being funny, that was it. Crowshaw found the levity offensive, assuming as it did a familiarity that must come from Freer's lack of confidence in Crowshaw's ability.

'I'll go and see her myself,' said Crowshaw. He had never liked Freer, and now he was beginning to understand why.

He rang down for his car and I left half a cup of tea in order to take him to the Gaines residence. Crowshaw said nothing to me on the way. It was a fine November afternoon that made it difficult to recall the previous fortnight's rain. The roads had dried under the warm sun.

Crowshaw admits that at that time he was painfully aware that this was his first murder, and that it was going wrong. Somehow the nature of a murder case always demands special attention to detail. It's not necessary to adduce a motive—though this one was obvious—only to prove the guilt. But a murder has to be sewn up with every detail neatly in place, and he knew that this thing was still awful ragged round the edges.

The Beeches was hidden from the road. We drove in beneath a heavily overhung belt of massive trees. The drive at that time went straight on past what was the front of the house, and I parked in a paved yard in front of a row of converted stables. Gaines's Morris Minor was in there, and a Rover 100 saloon which I supposed belonged to Mrs Gaines.

Crowshaw said I should go along with him and take notes, which was a bit of promotion, I suppose, due to him being annoyed with Freer. I tagged along, and we eventually found her in the garden.

Myra Gaines was pruning her roses, or at least snipping off the dead flowers. She stood in a blue cotton dress and a kind of smock against a back-cloth of blue, distant hills and a tumbled layer of landscaping down to a brook in the valley. I guessed her age as the late twenties, so I wasn't far out, which made her eighteen years younger than her husband. She had an impulsive, almost aggressive beauty, which I'd got time to appreciate while Crowshaw did the talking.

'Mr Crowshaw, isn't it?'

'I felt I ought to see you.'

She had a small wheelbarrow half full of ruined heads. 'Don't you think it's a sad time of year?' she asked.

'But it's a fine day.'

She looked at him quickly, half frowning. Her eyes were brown, far apart, level and unflinching. The brow was wide and smooth, with a high hairline, and at that time she wore her hair longer. Crowshaw found himself wondering whether her husband had ever attempted to capture some of her beauty on canvas, but certainly he could never seize and hold such a fluid flow of emotions as ran across her features. No still picture of her could record more than one of an infinite variety of poses. The impression was that she controlled her expression consciously, that she intended every second of it. Myra Gaines was a woman who played for attention, and she was enjoying being interviewed.

Then she smiled. 'There's very little I can add to what I told the sergeant.'

'I'm finding it rather difficult to understand your husband,' said Crowshaw. 'Of course, this was impulse. But it's not like the grabbing of a knife in a blind fury. It must have taken him twenty minutes to drive over to Paterson's. It suggests a settled anger, some sort of determination that he'd built himself up to.'

She inclined her head. Her secateurs went snip, snip, and two more soggy heads fell into the wheelbarrow.

'And I've talked with him a lot, now,' went on Crowshaw. 'He isn't the type to sustain such a pitch of emotion.'

'But he did,' she suggested gently.

'He's a quiet man, withdrawn—'

She caught at the word. 'Withdrawn!' Then the sound she made could have been a laugh or maybe a sob. 'Neville's in another world.' She moved her chin in an upward arc that hinted at anger. 'Withdrawn from existence, from all reality.'

'But *this* was real enough.'

Then she relaxed. The hand with the secateurs moved in despair. 'I never believed he could face anything. If I'd *believed* it, the whole thing might not have happened. I don't let myself think about that. But if I'd accepted he *could*, I'd have ... I don't know ... been prepared, perhaps.'

'The quiet men,' he said, 'build up inside and you can't see it, until they must face what they're trying not to see. And then the explosion carries them on and on ... until it's done.'

She was looking at him in anger. On that smooth brow her frown was a mere crimpling of the surface. 'Then why did you come here, if you understood?'

Crowshaw smiled. 'But I didn't, you see. You're helping me. You stimulate my imagination.'

It pleased her. 'Perhaps you'd better see his studio,' she said, as though it might offer more stimulation.

And a quiet man, he realized as he followed her, would be sustained by a rumbling fury at the disturbance to the gentle flow of his life. But would he sustain it as long as Gaines had? There was not just the long drive through the rain, and the subsequent hunt, but the prior preparation of approaching Lovejoy and buying the gun, and, now that the idea was growing in credibility, the approaching of somebody else and buying another.

She took us to the left from the terrace. Along this side of the house was a large glasshouse, built against the main structure as an annexe.

'My father grew tropical plants in here,' she explained.

It was hot and humid inside, though the greenery was then confined to one end and along one side. It was perhaps forty feet long and fifteen wide, the glazed walls rising up from ground level and continuing up in one sweep of curve, over to meet the house wall. It could hardly have been more unsuitable as an artist's studio, the sun slanting through the draped vines in a shimmering of green and gold light. Gaines had made an impractical attempt to control the light with shades, but there was such a conglomeration of cords that they'd become tangled long ago, and shades were stuck here and there so that the floor was mottled in a frantic distortion of light and shade. He had six easels scattered around the floor space, as though he had sprung from one to the other as the light changed and the inspiration seized him. Five had half-finished canvases on them, and on a table were his palette and brushes. No—no brushes, I saw; one palette knife only. And scattered about were the battered tubes of colour he had mangled in his strong fingers.

In the far corner a fountain played, its basin overflowing into a lower basin, and so on, down to a small pool in which several goldfish swam. Along the rear glass wall was a roof-high rack stacked with finished works. A dozen or so were leaning against it, drying it seemed.

'You can see how good he was,' she murmured, and Crowshaw detected sarcasm. His taste and knowledge of painting were both rudimentary. He knew what he liked, and he did not like these. Gaines had lashed at his canvases, scattering them with colour as though he hated them.

The place was fantastic, tumbled and untidy—Neville Gaines's refuge. For most people the house and grounds would have been sufficiently remote as a retreat from the hammerings of life. But here he had built the ultimate in

refuge, of such fantasy that he would be removed completely from all reality.

They had been married now for ten years. There was
one daughter, sent to stay with an aunt until it was all over.

'Neville was hopeless with everything,' Myra said, and
there was just a touch of fondness in her voice. She caught
Crowshaw's eye on her and laughed softly. 'I suppose that
was why I married him. I mean, you get so tired of people
fussing over you with their silly platitudes.'

I was watching a goldfish idly waving a tail against the
weak current. You couldn't imagine Myra becoming tired
of compliments, which was obviously what she meant. But
her husband, by inference, had not been free with his
platitudes. He'd be too introspective even to consider com-
plimenting anybody. He would present a singular challenge.

But Myra had taken on more than she could handle.
Gaines was self-centred, yes. He was inoffensive, certainly.
But he knew where he stood and how he intended to live.
He was so unpractical that he'd raised it to a fine art. The
changing of a razor blade became a performance of obscene
mutterings and eventual bleats for help.

'He can dress himself and feed himself,' Myra conceded
with a shrug. 'Though he was as difficult as hell. If we had
company I had to fight him into a decent suit, and he'd
sit at the table in one of his dazes, pretending he didn't
know one knife from the other. Just to embarrass me.'

She was moving around, picking things up and putting
them down. The studio was obviously as he'd walked out
of it. For a moment it seemed she was not going to continue.

'Perhaps he was simply absent-minded,' Crowshaw
prompted.

'No,' she said violently. 'He just could not understand
anything practical. Why, it took him three years to learn

to drive, and that was only when I refused to drive him myself.'

'Refused?'

'I had to do something. He was digging further and further into his shell. But, d'you know, even now he can't change gear without looking at the knob to see where the next notch is.'

Crowshaw nodded, smiling in sympathy.

'Even his painting,' she cried, picking up his palette knife. 'He got it all down to this. One knife. He used to slash on the colours with this thing, and you wouldn't believe the agony that went on before he could get himself to do it. He'd go into a daze, prowl around—and you couldn't get a word through. Then he'd pounce on the canvas and for five minutes it'd be splash and slash and flick—you'd have laughed, really you would. And the poor dear never realized it was rubbish.'

I'd been doing a tour of the easels. Her voice, in the background, was breaking towards the end. They were hideous, I thought, all crude colour and no taste, no form.

'The Royal Academy laughed at him,' she said, her voice now under control. 'The critics ignored him. But d'you think he cared. Not Neville. He just went along with his little life, and nothing I could do would shake him out of it.'

'But you tried?'

'I tried.' She glanced at him. 'I felt ... oh, I don't know. As though he was slipping from me, getting further and further out of touch all the time.'

There could be four hundred canvases there. Gaines might have been hopeless, but if they hanged him they'd sell as masterpieces. Gaines might be ironically pleased at the thought.

Crowshaw slipped it in very casually. 'And you don't

think he could re-load an automatic pistol?' he asked.

'What?'

He couldn't have expected such a startled response. The blood ran from her face and her eyes flickered.

'A technicality,' he explained. 'There were more shots than one gun-load, you might say.'

'That's ... oh, that's ridiculous.'

'His re-loading it?'

'He just couldn't.' She moved a hand, dismissing it.

'Too unpractical? Has he *ever* loaded one, do you know?'

'Neville couldn't fill a fountain pen.' And she instantly caught her lower lip between her teeth.

'But he could certainly fire the thing.'

'Yes ... I suppose so. I don't know,' she cried, her eyes bright. 'I don't want to think about it.'

'I can't help thinking about it.'

'No.' She looked at him with scorn, then immediately softened. 'It's your job, I suppose.'

'Did you know he'd got it?' I noticed he used the singular.

'The gun?' She beat her right fist into her other palm and walked away from him. 'Yes, I knew.'

'Yet you let him go?'

'Let him? How ... how would I know where he was going?'

'But you knew he'd bought a gun?'

'Andy Paterson told me. It was ridiculous.'

'And how did *he* know?'

Her eyes flickered. It had never occurred to her to wonder. 'I don't know.'

And that, I thought, was probably true.

'Ridiculous, you said,' Crowshaw prompted.

Her lips moved in a sad little smile. 'How else could Andy take it? Certainly not seriously.'

'Maybe he should have done.'

'That was his fault,' she cried. 'Neville's.' Emotion was crumbling her control. 'The way he'd arranged things. *His* fault.' Then it all came tumbling out as she tried to justify the claim, and Crowshaw let her get on with it.

She had made numerous attempts to draw him out, all unsuccessful. It seemed that he treated her overtures as a game, tossing the ball back at her happily. Any lure, bribe or threat only had an adverse effect; he simply retreated even deeper into his personal seclusion. He was insisting on being carried through life, and of course Myra resented it. She hated being taken for granted, and she felt he was leaving her behind on his personal journey to somewhere she could not reach. But Neville assumed she should be pleased, even happy, to bear the burden created by his Art. Angry frustration drove her on and on, in a pathetic search for some personal recognition. If he'd only *looked* at her, really looked! But he seemed not to understand her. She could not frighten him with threats of financial hardship. He sold nothing, but she had money, so what did it matter?

If his justification was in his painting, he must have considered hers was in protecting him from the harshness of life, so that more and more of his precious Art could burst into lurid life, even if it never reached an adoring public.

Into such an arid relationship there entered Andy Paterson. There would have to be an Andy Paterson some time.

Here Myra faltered, as though embarrassed. But it was merely because she was uncertain how to present Paterson.

'Andy never was a farmer at heart,' she said at last. 'I met him at a dance, over at the Darnley's. He was a big man —big, you understand, more than just size. He swept over you with that laugh of his, and with his confidence. Nothing was ever sacred to Andy, no private thought or secret...'

She paused. '... longing.' She glanced at Crowshaw, pro-
jecting her longing for companionship and affection,
reaching for his sympathy.

But would the longing have been such a secret? She
would have shrieked aloud her yearning, with every gesture
and every word.

Before very long she and Andy Paterson were spending
two or three evenings together.

'We went to concerts in Birmingham, shows, the ballet.
Once we did a trip down to London for the opera.'

'Did your husband know?' Crowshaw asked.

'I kept nothing from him.' She was proud, defiant. 'Do
you imagine he'd care?'

'I don't know.' Crowshaw considered it. 'I imagine so.'

'Then he never showed it,' she flashed back.

Neville had presented a flat indifference. He was unmoved to hear that she was spending evenings at Paterson's
place. He didn't seem to believe it. So she brought Paterson
home and showed him to Neville, if only to prove his
existence.

Antagonism bristled at the meeting. Andy was patroniz-
ing and hearty. He flung out inferences that should have
shrivelled Neville's complacency, but only increased his
polite disdain. Paterson he plainly considered a heathen.
The evening ended with a singular triumph for Neville's
quiet contempt. And later, when Andy had gone, there was
a hysterical outburst from Myra, from which Neville quietly
walked into his studio.

It lasted six months. Neville would not believe. Though
she stayed late at Paterson's farm, Neville would not be
shaken. Myra had too much taste, he inferred.

'And had you?' Crowshaw asked.

She flashed hatred at him. 'I loved Andy.'

'And he loved you?' he asked softly.

She bathed in it. Recalling, she moved sensually.

'Yes, Andy loved me.'

But Paterson had become intensely possessive. It mattered little to him whether her husband knew, realized, accepted —or just disappeared in a puff of smoke. Paterson simply hated Gaines for his contempt and his indifference.

Several times he invited both of them to the farm. It gave him hearty pleasure to flaunt his feelings under Neville's nose. But every visit ended with Paterson burning in fury, and Neville's calm eyes never seeing anything but a heathen.

In the end Myra had grown tired of it. Andy's possessiveness had become wearisome, and it had all been a failure. She had only wanted to jerk Neville into reality. Really, it had always been that, she told Crowshaw. But Andy would not release her. His hold was a social one. Myra moved— usually without Neville—in a social circle which she prized. Andy could ruin that for her, by always being there with remarks and suggestions calculated to ruin her reputation, which up to that time he had respected. Abruptly she became afraid of him.

Neville seemed as unmoved by her fear of Paterson as he had been by her apparent attraction to him. There was a terrible scene, when she tried to express her fear of Andy, and her inability to avoid seeing him. But Neville saw it as yet another challenge. She screamed, wept, at his in-difference—and Neville simply walked away into his studio.

Then there was one final visit—Neville and herself—to the farm. She hoped to provoke Neville into some sort of demand, however feeble, that Paterson should never see her again. And Neville calmly walked out into the soft September evening, leaving them together over their drinks.

Myra was drunk when he drove her home. Neville said nothing.

Crowshaw waited while she collected herself. The soft scatter of the fountain dwelt on the air. Her voice was hoarse.

'Then Andy phoned to say that Neville had bought a gun. He was laughing about it. I didn't know what it meant. I just couldn't ask Neville. You understand. It was a joke ... or something. I didn't guess. How *could* I have guessed?'

But something had happened to Neville Gaines, because he took that gun up to Paterson's farm, and solved the problem for good and all. And if Myra could understand it, she was now certainly too upset to express anything but anguish.

I could see that Crowshaw realized there was nothing further to be gained by staying, so shortly afterwards we left.

The sun was low on the drive back, and dreary streaks of mist snaked across the road between the high hedges, seeping down from the fields. Crowshaw didn't say a word.

I went off home, but Crowshaw wasn't so lucky. Freer had gone off duty. On Crowshaw's desk were the evening papers, and they weren't encouraging. They complained there were no official claims of progress on the case. What was holding things up? Crowshaw threw them from him in anger.

There was a curt note from the Chief Super's office, requesting his presence early in the morning. He went down to see Gaines, viewing him now with fresh eyes—but he saw nothing new. Sympathized, perhaps, but did not understand.

'Have you seen a solicitor?' he asked.

'He came this afternoon.' Gaines sounded unimpressed.

He was spread on his bunk, and made no move to rise. Crowshaw took the single hard chair.

'What did he say?'

'Not to tell you anything.' Well at least he was frank. 'But there's no more to say, is there?'

Crowshaw said: 'I'm not supposed to advise you. I'm not even supposed to be seeing you now, not alone. I've just been to see your wife.'

Interest flickered in Neville's weary eyes. 'How was she?'

'She said you couldn't have re-loaded the gun.' Crowshaw watched him, but there was none of the anticipated reaction. 'Either you took two guns with you—'

'No. No, I'm ... sure I didn't.'

'Or you re-loaded.'

Gaines turned slowly to look at him. 'Why should I help you? I've admitted it. Isn't that enough?'

'Far from it. Dozens of people admit to crimes. We have to prove it.'

'Then go ahead and prove it.'

The solicitor had been smart after all. He'd seen the significance of the extra shots. Was Gaines sensing a way out?

'We may have to drop the case.'

Gaines levered himself on to one elbow. 'Drop it?'

'Tell the Magistrate we don't want to pursue it. You'd be discharged.'

'You're being very frank.'

'Because you won't admit to two guns.' Then he went on casually: 'Why did you ask Lovejoy specifically for a thirty-eight automatic?'

Gaines stared. 'That's what they're called, isn't it?'

Oh good Lord, so Freer had been so nearly right.

'And you went round Birmingham hunting for thirty eights?'

'Only one.' Gaines lifted his head in challenge. 'One.'

'Then you *must* have re-loaded that one.'

But Crowshaw had lost him. Gaines was tired of it.

'Perhaps I did. If you say so.'

'No—you do. You say you killed him. Then you must have re-loaded, or you must have had two.'

Gaines shrugged, and Crowshaw left him to think about it.

In the morning he went straight down to see Gaines, and found him about to shave. He threw down on the bunk the thirty-eight that Gaines had bought from Lovejoy, and a handful of rimless cartridges.

'All right, show me. It's empty. You load it.'

Gaines slowly wiped lather from his face. He came over to the bunk. 'It's a joke?'

'No. You load that thing if you think you can.' He twisted his mouth. 'Then you can blast your way out of here.'

Gaines gave him an uncertain smile. He picked up the gun and turned it over in his hand, and looked up at Crowshaw as though for guidance. He was so confused that Crowshaw was certain he didn't know which would benefit him most, to succeed or to fail. Then he flicked the safety catch on and off, and jerked back the chamber.

'Lovejoy showed me that,' he said.

But he had no idea where the magazine was. He raised his eyebrows at Crowshaw. 'You win.'

'Or lose—perhaps.' Crowshaw scooped it all into his pocket and turned to go.

'Oh ... while you're here...' It was such a meek little smile. 'Could you perhaps ... change the blade in my razor?'

'Oh, you're good,' said Crowshaw. 'Good.' But all the same he changed the blade.

When he got up there, the Chief Super's attitude was unmistakable. 'What's holding you?' he asked bleakly.

Crowshaw explained stolidly, through all the interruptions.

'He's faking,' said his chief.

'No, sir. There's too much circumstantial evidence. I'll swear he didn't know how to re-load the thing.'

'Then it leaves you with one alternative.'

'I know. A second gun.' Crowshaw paused. 'There's something convinces me he *had* got two guns. Something he slipped out, sir. He said, about not having two: "I'm sure." As though he really wasn't, and it was worrying him.'

'We'll have to bring him before the Magistrate. Do you want me to ask for an adjournment?'

'It may not be necessary.' Crowshaw looked at his fingers. 'A dozen men, sir. Twenty. I'll find that other gun before Monday. It's got to be somewhere, in all that mud.'

He looked up into doubtful eyes. There was a long pause. Then: 'Twenty men, Crowshaw. And get it by Monday.'

On Saturday morning it began to rain again. I recall that Crowshaw simply saw it as an extra challenge. He was in a fighting mood. We took twelve men from HQ, and met eight they'd provided from neighbouring local stations. I was one of the twelve. Four went on a general search of the farm area, in case that damned second gun was lying somewhere in the open. The rest of us were on mud detail.

'It's not going to be pleasant,' Crowshaw told us. 'That gun could have been trodden down under a foot of mud. Very nasty. But the sooner it's found, the sooner we can pack it in and get round to the pub for a few drinks.'

We had it quartered with string on pegs and ran the operation like a military campaign. Freer supervised. Crowshaw waited in the Cambridge.

I drew the pig sty. Freer wouldn't let us hurry, and I

recall it as a special portion of hell. The job had to be done well. Inch by inch. We searched the byres and the sty and the compost heaps, shoulder deep in stench. The rain never ceased. The day began with sardonic humour, deteriorated to grumbles, and ended in near-revolt. We found three more shell cases, but no gun.

Crowshaw burned with a slow fury. I drove him back, and could sense him smouldering.

I didn't know it then, but he went back alone on the Sunday morning, and tramped morosely about the farm. Drover accompanied him, silently and in mute sympathy.

'You ever meet him?' Crowshaw asked at one point.

'Gaines? Once or twice. Funny chap.'

And Crowshaw wondered where a funny chap might have thrown his second gun.

On Monday morning he went to the Chief Super's office without any summons. He was so dispirited that he was close to asking to be taken off the case. The Chief Constable was there.

'No luck, I hear.'

Crowshaw looked at him doubtfully. The CC was a bluff man in his middle sixties. He had no patience with failure. No luck, indeed!

'We didn't find it.'

His thin smile indicated the strain on the CC's composure. 'We can't afford failure.'

'It's there,' Crowshaw burst out. 'I know it's there.'

'But you've searched,' the CC said quietly. He held up his hand. 'Now look, even assuming he had two guns, he could have taken one right away. Perhaps thrown it into the Severn.'

'No sir. He isn't the sort for that. He just threw the other one down, so he'd just throw this one down.'

'But he didn't,' snapped the Chief Supt.

The CC's eyes never moved. 'Well?'

Crowshaw took a breath. 'You'd need to see what it's like up there. You've never seen such conditions. There's every likelihood that we missed it.'

'You believe?'

'I'm sure. I'd stake anything—'

Again the thin smile. 'You might well be doing that.'

Crowshaw saw the invitation dangled before him. Now was the time to withdraw. Let another man sweat, a senior man. But if he failed again... 'I want to try again, sir.'

The Chief Super exploded. 'Why the hell...' He stopped dead at the CC's raised hand.

'Let him say it.'

Crowshaw clasped one palm on each of his spread knees. 'I'm certain he couldn't re-load. I'm certain he'd got hold of another gun. There was something in the way Lovejoy spoke, as though Gaines had asked for two thirty-eights. Lovejoy could have passed him on to another supplier, but he wouldn't dare say. I can't imagine why he'd want two guns, but there *is* a little something about that. When I questioned Gaines I asked him about the seven shots in one gun being enough, and he reacted strangely, as though perhaps they weren't. No sir, I think he bought two guns, and now he's wise to the fact that if he denies it there could be a way out for him.' He drew a breath. 'Let me try again, sir, with a different set of men.'

'You mean you think one of them missed it?'

'One of them,' said Crowshaw, 'must have missed it.'

The CC drew patterns on the Chief Super's blotter, whilst Crowshaw stared woodenly out of the window at the grey sky. At last the heavy head came up. 'Very well. We'll try it again.' He lifted his hand. 'But Crowshaw ... don't fail again.'

They got an adjournment at the Magistrate's court, and

Gaines's solicitor seemed satisfied. But the Chief Constable was a man who knew when the time had come for the buck to be firmly passed. He called a Press Conference. By Tuesday morning the papers were pulsing with it, and Crowshaw realized that he was being set up. Somebody had got to try this important throw of the dice, and if that somebody was going to fail and be pitched into the depths, it was better that it should be Crowshaw rather than his CC.

The newspapers had found a double-ended personal-interest story ready made. On the one side, the guilt of Neville Gaines, on the other the career of an untried Chief Inspector, both hanging on the discovery or otherwise of an automatic pistol.

On the Thursday Crowshaw tried again. The farm was swarming with newsmen and cameramen. Crowshaw cursed them, and kept them at a distance. He worked to the same pattern as before, each man assigned a specific area, but with forty men this time and a clear sky above them. This time they worked slower. Crowshaw sat in the back of the Austin Cambridge, and waited. I sat in the front and waited, because I'd had my go.

At two-thirty on that first day there was a shout. The sergeant came running. 'In the cow byre,' he panted. 'By God, you were right.'

Crowshaw looked at the slimy gun in Freer's hand.

'I was right.'

We drove away at once, leaving Freer to clear up. They had heard at HQ, and they swarmed round the car, slapping his shoulders as he climbed out. 'By heaven, you must feel good.'

Thirteen years later he admitted that in fact he felt terrible.

We had long since finished the sandwiches and the tea.

'If the second gun had been found as soon as the first,' said Crowshaw, 'Gaines might have stood a chance.'

It was honest of him to say so. I nodded.

'I hadn't wanted all the publicity,' he explained. 'But when somebody takes a set of facts and from them deduces an expected result, and that result crops up in a blaze of publicity, then it's apt to weigh heavily.'

'But it's hardly something I can take to his widow,' I said. 'You're saying he may have got away with something less? Justification ... that sort of thing.'

We were tossing it around, two ex-policemen reminiscing, and me hoping he'd take the tray back so that I could turn that magazine over. But he didn't. He got to his feet.'

'I'm sorry it's been such a waste of your time.'

'Not at all.' I turned at the door. 'One thing...'

'Yes?'

'Why didn't you trace back the second gun?'

He raised his eyebrows. 'Hardly necessary, was it?' He smiled. The pupils of his eyes had narrowed to pin-points, but he wasn't looking into the sun.

I left him. He didn't come round the house with me, so I got a look at the dark shape in the barn. It was an oldish Jaguar, dark blue, so battered he might have been using it as a tractor.

While I was at it, I took a look in the cow byre, where they'd found the second gun. Not much had been done to clear the floor of stale mud and straw and manure, and it was still sloppy from a leak in the roof. It was dark in there.

I got back in the Porsche and in a couple of miles I was feeling a bit more relaxed. But there was still an uneasy prickling in the back of my neck. Crowshaw had calmly and deliberately told me more than he needed to have done.

It was ten to four when I reached Elsa's.

CHAPTER SIX

She'd got tea laid on, with tomato sandwiches and toasted teacake. I didn't mention I'd already had tomato sandwiches. I was feeling a bit edgy. But Elsa bubbled and fluttered. She was excited, though why she should get all worked up about marrying Dave Mallin I couldn't understand. Looking at her, I could see that Dave Mallin had every reason to be excited. But I wasn't. As I say, I was edgy.

Then afterwards we played some records, and things got round to the point where I'd either have to stay the night or leave there and then.

'We're getting married on Friday,' she said. 'Da ... vid!'

Did I say I wasn't excited?

I got back to my place about eleven, and don't remember climbing the stairs, and at ten the next morning I was in Wolverhampton, looking for somewhere to park. I found a car park by the market and walked up from there to the square, and found Fiston & Greene in a little cul-de-sac by the church. Mr Greene would see me if I'd wait a minute. He saw me in ten.

He had a bright, shining, modern office, when I'd expected something fusty. Greene was himself fusty, but he was trying to do something about it. The chair he sat me in was moulded from one sheet of ply, and designed to speed the unwelcome client.

Mr Greene said: 'Mr ... er ... er?'

I told him I was investigating the death of a young man

called Paul Hutchinson. A little distress grew in those tired
old eyes. He reached up and ruffled the hair over his ears.

'He's dead?'

'A car accident.'

'I'm very sorry.'

I explained. I was an enquiry agent, I told him, and
my enquiries had led me to believe Paul had been his
client.

'Mr Mallin, if there's any reason to query the death of
my client, I might be prepared to discuss it with the police.'

'He was my client, too, and I'm discussing it with you.'

The barest hint of a smile. 'Hardly the same, is it?'

'I'm not sure I like my clients dying on me,' I told him.

'Your fee? Perhaps the estate—'

'Will cover yours, yes. I'm not asking it to cover mine.'

I'd ruffled him. He touched his desk calendar with one
finger and hummed a bit.

'If you'd state your business, then.'

'You wrote to him a couple of months ago. You said you
enclosed his father's letter. That letter may be important,
but it's missing. So I'm wondering if you've got a copy of it.'

'Hardly likely.'

'Or if you could tell me what it was about. Roughly.'

He looked all disapproving at his pen set. 'As to the circumstances,' he said, 'I can only tell you that Paul's father
committed suicide a matter of six months ago. An overdose
of sleeping pills, if I remember correctly. He left a letter
for his son. I kept no copy, but I can advise you, Mr
Mallin...' There was a cheeky twinkle in his eyes. '...
without fee, that the coroner's office will no doubt have
kept a copy of it.'

I wasn't going to get any more out of him. I thanked him,
advised him—without fee—to buy a more friendly chair,
and left.

I found the coroner's office on foot, and they turned out to be rather more helpful. They hadn't simply kept a copy, they let me see the photostat.

I copied it down on a sheet of paper they gave me, with a pen they'd lent me because I'd come without one. A fine detective I was!

Dear Paul,

I know you're going to blame me but I don't want you to so I'm writing you this, and I hope when you've read it you'll understand, because things are not all black and white and whatever they tell you, you don't want to take too much notice of. When you read this you'll understand you can't put a finger on it and say this is it or that is it, and that's the answer. I'm not putting this right. Before I started writing it was all clear in my head, what I wanted to say, but somehow all I can see is that sloppy bewildered look of yours, and all I want is for you not to be bewildered. But you know how it's been with me, and all I've had to hold on to is how you're doing so well in that job, but that's not enough because a man's got his pride. You've always got to remember that Paul that a man's got his pride, and it's the facing of it over and over that gets you down. Just the people looking at you and seeing in their eyes that they know, and it's no good you coming along with your how can they possibly know, because they do, and that's that. So with this last job only lasting a fortnight and all, I knew there wasn't any good carrying on. And that's the truth of it.

I want you to know the truth of it. Whatever they say, son, I searched that place. Really searched. Nobody could have done any better. Didn't I find those three shell cases for them? So I must have looked well and proper. That's all I want to say.

I've just read this over, and it doesn't half say what

I want to say. But it's just so you'll understand, son.
Don't hold it against me.
    Your loving,
        Dad.

You could read in parts of the letter that he'd certainly
had an obsession. I was reminded of Karen's feeling that
everybody saw her as the daughter of Neville Gaines, murderer.

I thanked them and went away. 'Them' was a creamy
blonde who'd got the deepest blue eyes I've ever seen, and
I'd have her name for you only I was getting married on
Friday.

I had landed on a market day, so the traffic was bad. I
edged my way round the block a few times, and eventually
found my way on to the island and out to the road for
Shrewsbury. Then I made good time, driving fast as
though something was chasing me. Something was. I didn't
like to think how that letter might have affected Paul.

I made it in forty minutes. They'd improved the Police
HQ buildings since I'd been there. You couldn't expect
them to stand still, simply because I'd chosen to transfer.
I asked for Freer. Yes, he was still with them, a Det. Chief
Inspector now. But he was out on a case. Would I care to
wait? What else could I do? I filled in by doing a wander
round to see if any of my old mates were still there. One or
two were, just where they'd been twelve years before, so
their ribbing about my present job left me quite unmoved.

Freer came in at last. He was snappily dressed and
carried a zipped document case under his arm. He still
walked with vigorous dignity, not looking to right or left.
He was thinner and more supercilious, his cynicism having
soured. He wouldn't have been a popular man to work for.

Eventually I got in to see him. They'd had a hi-jacking

on the A5 the night before, and Freer was up to his neck
in it. He said he'd give me ten minutes. To him I was a
minor constable from an unimportant corner of his past,
and he just wasn't interested.

'Mallin?' he said. 'Yes, I remember.'

There was nothing relaxed about him. He leaned forward in his chair like a cat about to strike, and waited, not
prompting.

'You'll perhaps remember the Paterson murder?' I
asked. It wasn't important to him, because he hadn't been
in charge. His eyes were steady. He said nothing.

'You were a sergeant,' I prodded him.

His lips curled. 'You've got a nice regard for rank.'

'You were my hero.'

Something dark stirred behind his eyes. 'And you came
back after twelve years to tell me so?'

'To ask if you remember the Paterson murder.'

'Of course I do.'

'At the time,' I said, 'I was a driver. But nothing important, like sergeant.'

'You are now, then?'

'Now I'm a private enquiry agent.'

'Ah! Divorce and things like that.'

'Not so far,' I admitted. 'Nothing worse than murder.'

'Andrew Paterson's murder? You're a bit late for that.'

'Something more recent. The murder of a young man,
and his father's suicide.'

'I haven't got much time.'

'I wanted to ask you about the father.'

'And you think I'd know?'

'You've got a good memory. That search,' I said. 'You'll
remember that first time we searched for the second gun.
We didn't find it.'

He smiled. The corners of his mouth moved outwards

but not upwards. It was painful to watch. 'Yes, of course.
You were in on that. As you say, you didn't find it.'

'I drew the pig sty.'

'Very unfortunate.'

'But who,' I asked, 'was Hutchinson?'

I actually caught him unawares. There was not much to
show but a flicker of the eyelashes, and the very slight
pause before he said:

'One of the men.'

'On the first search?'

'Yes.' He was obviously back in his official shell.

'Where on the first search?'

It was probably unusual for him to be on the receiving
end of questions. He didn't like it. 'The cow byre.'

So I'd guessed right. 'On his own?'

'I decided it wasn't too much for one man.'

'So you blame yourself?'

'For what?' So polite—so deadly.

'For putting him in there alone.'

'Not at all.'

'But on the second search, that's where it was. Maybe
he missed it because it was all too much for him.'

'I told you,' he said calmly, 'I'd decided it was not.'

'Afterwards?' I asked.

'At the time.'

'But afterwards, what happened,' I insisted.

I could see he wasn't going to let me carry on much
longer. Only by keeping the knife in and digging at him
could I hope to get through to the end. Pride wouldn't
let him send me away.

'To Hutchinson?' He slightly lifted his shoulders. 'He
was dismissed.'

Somehow I kept the incredulity from my voice. 'For missing the gun?'

'He didn't find it, did he?'

I slid on to another tack. 'He wasn't from HQ, was he?'

'No. He was from one of the country beats.'

'Or I'd have heard about it,' I explained.

He picked up a pencil and considered it with concentration. 'It would hardly be your affair.' He looked along it. Perhaps it was bent.

'But somewhere along the line it'd be yours. The gun was missed, that first search. So somebody had to suffer.'

'Mr Crowshaw would naturally have to put in a report. Really, Mallin...'

It was the first crack; he was protesting.

'And he'd pass it back to you. And you'd say you'd considered it wasn't too much for one man. So back it went to Hutchinson. Then it stopped. Just a country copper. Nowhere for him to pass it. What did you say happened to him?'

The skin was white around his nostrils. 'He was dismissed.'

'For missing the gun?'

'What's it got to do with you?'

I was upset. I admit it. 'He committed suicide.' My voice was too loud.

'What's the connection?'

'I don't know,' I shouted. 'I don't bloody-well know.'

The smile creaked. 'Then I suggest you go away and find out.' Then at last he got round to it. 'And now, I'm afraid, I'll have to ask you to leave.'

'I know—you're very busy.'

'As always.'

I left him and his thin smile and went out to the Porsche. One or two of the boys were round it, a strange car in their car park. 'This yours, Dave?' I said it was. They nodded approval. 'It's what you get on this private enquiry racket,'

one of them commented. I told them it's what you get for
marrying a woman with money.

So—back to Wolverhampton. Two-goes-at-a-job Mallin
they call me. I had difficulty parking this time and had to
walk half across town. They were pleased to see me at the
coroner's office, and I did what I should have done the first
time. I read it all.

Most of the meat came in Paul's own evidence. He'd
grown up with it. His father had been dismissed from the
force six months after Neville Gaines was convicted. This
father, you could get the picture, wasn't a tough character
by any means. No resilience. It had hit him low. He'd tried
to build up a detective agency, but the people who'd go
to an ex-cop who'd been thrown out would be apt to expect
somebody not too honest. Or maybe he didn't try hard
enough. Anyway, it drifted on for two years, then Hutchinson was on the labour market again. A policeman doesn't
get any technical training that's any use in a factory. He
tried labouring. As I say, he wasn't tough enough. One job
drifted on to the next, with always the mounting feeling
that his dismissal was haunting him, chasing him from one
failure to the next.

Paul had been about sixteen when his mother died. I
got the impression she just gave up. Poppa Hutchinson
dragged on. There were incidents. A fight or two—Hutchinson claiming somebody had sneered at him. Very soon it
wasn't just the lack of money that drove him—he and his
son—from rented rooms to bed-sitters; there were neigh-
bours in whom Hutchinson was certain to detect a knowledge of his past failings. Then they'd have to leave. Paul
said in evidence that he was at seven schools in six years.
But he'd been a brainy lad, and his ability had at last
provided him with the means to make his own life, apart
from his father.

You could see, from Paul's statement, that he had been very uneasy—even guilty—about leaving his father to carry on alone. But he'd had as much as he could handle. Towards the end Hutchinson was attempting to retain work at a factory as a nightwatchman. As his letter indicated, the last job didn't go on for long, and it was all the man could take. His obsession had for some time been robbing him of sleep, and his doctor had had him on sedatives. Enough of these had been left to do the job.

I handed all the stuff in and left. Oh—I got her name for you. Daphne. She said she was free that evening, and I told her I was getting married on Friday. She pointed out it was only Wednesday, so I got out of there fast.

I was away from the kerb before I'd decided what to do. Birmingham, and a quiet evening with the tele? You're joking. Shropshire and The Beeches—or to Elsa? I didn't want to see anybody such as Elsa. Nobody I liked. I had a desire to meet somebody I could kick in the teeth. Yet it was too early for Finn at The Beeches.

Paul Hutchinson had been killed for his father's letter and to keep him quiet. Something he'd said or inferred had given somebody the wrong idea. He hadn't got any intention of shaking-up that old case. Hadn't he said something to Myra about where the second gun was found being important? It was—to Paul. Because it'd been found where his father had searched. No, he hadn't been interested in who killed whom and why, all he'd wanted was a way of getting back at Crowshaw, who'd had his father dismissed with a snap of the fingers, when the poor chap had really done his best.

I'm an economical type myself. I hate waste. Paul's death was waste. His father's was waste.

In the end I drove out and picked up the M6, and batted along there for an hour. It didn't do me any good, but it warmed the engine.

It wasn't as dark as I'd have wished when I got to The Beeches. Half a mile short of the entrance I found a pull-off by a bridge and eased the car in there out of sight. Then I continued on foot. At that time of the evening the car park would be empty, and I didn't want to dump the Porsche in the middle of a naked expanse of tarmac. On the way up the drive I kept well in under the trees. In the west the sky was still green and gold beneath a line of hard, purple cloud. The lights were dim in the ballroom and gaming room. I kept on straight up the side of the building, and round to the row of garages.

The first four were still locked. There was nothing in any of the others. So much for all my crafty work. I was walking away, treading even and gentle to cut down the sound, when it occurred to me that there was something not quite right. I'm not the thinking sort; I go by impressions and instincts. This was an instinct. I stopped. I turned.

I was standing exactly where I'd parked the Cambridge thirteen years before. Looking round, going by the glow left in the sky, I felt the feeling growing stronger. My memory is not for facts—I get mental pictures. Now I had a mental picture of how it had looked from the Cambridge, and something was different. After thirteen years, so what? I stood poised, and worried about it. Then I saw it.

The row of garages presented the appearance of a long, low building with a row of double doors down the length. But why was there a high double door inset into the end of the building? *That* hadn't been there before. I went to have a closer look. They were heavy doors, and there was a large padlock on them. The end garage therefore had two sets of doors, on adjacent walls.

I went back to the Porsche, keeping on the grass. I dug

it out with some difficulty, then drove openly up the drive and round to the parking lot. The floodlights weren't on. I slid the car in against the far fence, next to the only other car there.

When I got out I saw it was the dark grey Rover. Every thing was quiet, and by that time it was quite dark. One of these days I'll buy myself a torch. What I could detect by touch and the flash of my lighter spark, the blustering wind taking the flame off before it caught, indicated that somebody had been doing some work on it. There was no abrasion along the offside bonnet. There didn't seem to be any dent in the bumper.

I went on into the club. Dead and empty. No Feeney at the door. In the ballroom a couple of women were polishing the floor. Low and discreet lights from the walls were the only illumination. The women spoke in echoes. I went on through the curtains.

The bar was also dimly lit. No customers and no barman. The counter gleamed with polish. Behind it, Carter Finn and another man were standing with their backs to me, drinking scotch. A curtain makes very little sound opening. I allowed it to drift back into place with even less. Finn's companion was a bull of a man, his glass tiny in a hairy great hand. I trod gently. The phone booth was the other end of the bar.

'One seventy-five,' said Finn.

Bull-neck laughed. I'd know that bellowing, scornful low anywhere. 'A quid.'

I got opposite them, and smiled. 'Use your phone?' Then I sailed on past. The bull's face was heavy and jowled, sideboards low and luxuriant. He looked startled.

Inside the booth I found I hadn't got the sort of change you feed them with. I went out again to see if Finn could split me a fifty. His friend was gone. It had been so fast that the only place I could imagine for him was crouching under the bar. You could tell Finn wasn't pleased to see me. What'd he expect? You hire a private detective and he's apt to drop in any time. He bashed a key on the cash register, and the drawer flew open.

'What the hell you want round here?'

'Reporting in ... boss,' I said blandly.

He gave me change and watched me with controlled disgust. As I turned away: 'Use the one in the office.'

Which he'd got tapped? I leered at him. 'No thank you. But I'll put the call on your bill.'

Freer was still at his office. 'Oh, it's you again.'

'Listen, mate,' I said. 'I'm doing you a favour. Say the word, and I'll ring off.'

There was a minimal silence, then a shift in his tone when he got it out. 'All right. Sorry. What's up?'

'I'm at The Beeches. Finn's place. Know it?'

'I know it.' His voice was suddenly keen and sharp. 'That hi-jacking case you're on. Don't tell me...' He didn't. 'Was it whisky?'

'How'd you guess?'

'You're always waiting to pounce,' I complained. 'What sort of wagon?'

'An articulated,' he said. 'Loaded with the stuff.'

'Which you haven't found?'

'The thing can't have evaporated.'

I turned and looked out of the narrow glass door. Finn wasn't hovering. 'There's a row of garages here, the first four of them locked. There's another double door at the end. If somebody knocked down three separating walls they could back an artic into there and lock it away.'

'That'd be clever. This is a hunch, is it?'

'It was. But I've just seen Busoni here.'

We both knew Busoni very well. He operated from

London, but spread his net wide. Busoni would buy anything from anybody, never asked a question, and had mar-
kets so hidden that not even Scotland Yard had managed
to pin him down.

'I'll be right over,' said Freer.

'Better make it fast. Finn knows I've spotted Busoni.'

We didn't have time to say goodbye. The phone was
dead in my hand. I went out to thank Finn for his accom-
modating attitude, but he wasn't there. Nobody was there.

Just at that time I had every intention of telling Finn
that the investigation was a dud. Paul Hutchinson had
been chasing a revenge campaign against Crowshaw. There
was nothing in it for Finn or for Myra. I was getting
married on Friday, and I'd had enough of it. That was
what I was going to say. But he wasn't there. So I couldn't
tell him, could I?

I lit a cigarette and looked around. In the gaming room
the wheels were tidily clad in green baize nightdresses, and
the ghosts of happy losers laughed in the eerie silence. I
could go over there and through the door into the hall and
winkle out the Finns. But I didn't. The scotch had gone
from the bar, so I couldn't help myself to a drink. I wandered out to the car park.

The sun had called it a day and the black clouds had
closed down on the horizon. The blustery wind was picking
up cold. I threw away the cigarette and thought I'd do the
same as the sun.

One thing I hadn't tried. I tried it. To my surprise the
Rover's door was open. I reached in. A box of paper handkerchiefs in the glove compartment. I fumbled behind it
and my hand fell on a torch.

I hadn't been wrong. There was no dent in the bumper.
The wing was perfect. It wasn't just a fill-in and smooth-
over, but looked like a new wing. Fast work, if that was

the case. In the torchlight I couldn't detect any variation
in shade between the wing and the rest of the car. That's
where it usually shows; they never quite match the original
colour. A complete re-spray? Surely not. Nobody could
have done all that work in the time. I checked the number
plates, and I'd got the right car. But on this one the tyres
were Cinturatos. On the other they'd been Goodyears.

There wouldn't be any need to change the tyres, surely!
I crouched down low, checking. No, they hadn't changed
the tyres, they'd changed the whole bloody car.

Now, that really was smart work, and even faster than
a re-spray would be. But somebody had gone out with clear
instructions. A dark grey Rover 3 litre automatic, circa
1968. Get it, bring it in, switch the plates. Hell, Finn had
got some useful connections. And somewhere, deep in a
desolate ravine or in somebody's abandoned quarry, there'd
be lying the burnt-out wreck of a dark grey Rover, now
unrecognisable.

Finn was good. He was very good.

All I heard was the creak of leather as a shoe changed
emphasis, and the soft hiss of something heavy moving
through the air. I heard it because it finished up just above
my right ear.

CHAPTER SEVEN

I lay still awhile after consciousness returned, and thought about it. Not that I gained anything, except perhaps the time to get scared.

We were in a car. It was moving fast. There was a contented hum about the engine and a self-satisfied comfort in the upholstery that told me we were probably in the Rover. But there was a good chance I was on my way to join the other Rover, which might not yet be a burnt-out wreck. They probably wanted to make it look good with the burnt-out body of a driver inside.

I eased open one eye and surveyed the possibilities. On one side of me was Troy, just about obscuring the near-side window. We were in the back, and on the other side of me was somebody else I couldn't see, but could smell— aniseed. He was sucking aniseed sweets. Wedged between my thigh and Troy's was the box of paper handkerchiefs. He dug into them from time to time. Troy had the sniffs. It was too late to hope it might develop into pneumonia. The driver was just a heavy bulk between me and the wheel. That made three of them. I couldn't see much I could do with three.

Troy took another paper handkerchief. The floor around his feet was scattered with them. Then suddenly he shone a pencil light in my eyes and caught me in the middle of a frown.

'He's with us,' he told the other two.

'You might at least chuck 'em out of the window,' I said.

'What?'

'The handkerchiefs. It ain't hygienic.'

It struck him as funny. There were shaking movements from him, but no sound.

'It wasn't a good idea,' I told him.

The thing behind my right shoulder breathed aniseed all over me and grumbled: 'Shut him up, for Chrissake.' I'd know the voice again—and the breath.

'What wasn't?' said Troy.

'Switching the car. It's too obvious.'

'It was scratched, so it had to go.'

'Yes, I can see that.'

Troy was being affable, like offering me the best meal he could, just before the end. 'Traded it in,' he said smoothly.

I had a brief impression of streets crowding us. We were going through a town. There were lights beyond the windows.

'Nothing funny,' Troy said softly.

And just what, in the funny line, could I have done?

Then we were out of there and climbing. The box was dropping all the time into third, then into second when tight corners began to slow us.

'Here?' said the driver suddenly, and I felt my muscles bunch.

Troy peered ahead and behind. I could see now that the wipers were working. There wasn't anything but darkness out there.

'It'll do.'

I did what I could, but the space was confined. They didn't stop the car to give me more room, but did it on the move. Aniseed-breath mainly held me. Once or twice he cursed and added his fist when I managed to get in the odd blow; but that was at first. Then Troy justified my faith in him and got in a few short-arm jabs, so I was nearly unconscious when he started in with the gun.

He smashed my left hand with it, while his mate held it hard on the top edge of the front seat. It took him three hefty swings. Then at last, satisfied, they opened the nearside door and pitched me out.

We were doing around forty at the time, but fortunately we were close in, so that I hit grass. Wet grass. For a distance I slid along head first, then managed to scramble round for what I was sure to be going to hit, and went through the low, white fence with my feet. Then I went straight on, pitching and twisting down the slope beyond. Small gorse bushes slowed me. I stopped with my head beside a racing brook, with a rustling movement around me, and lay breathless under the sweet and gentle rain.

After a couple of minutes the car came past along the road in the opposite direction. I could just see the top, and the lights kicking into the rain. They did not stop to see if there was anything left of me to push around.

After a while I managed to force myself on to hands and knees. Steaming shapes moved around me in the darkness and one of them coughed gently. The sheep had come to see who was visiting.

I could not tell what had happened to my left hand, but it felt bad enough and looking at it wouldn't have helped. I didn't know the time. My watch is—was—luminous, but while he was at it Troy had smashed that too.

I decided to try the slope. On the way down it had seemed steep enough. On the way up it was near vertical. With only one hand and arm to drag myself with, and the short grass slimy with rain, I had difficulty making any progress at all. The gorse bushes helped, those I hadn't torn out on the way down. Every now and then I lay with a heel wedged against the stubble of bush, and rested.

Then I had another go at it.

I reached the white fence. It occurred to me that some-body's sheep were going to be wandering out of the hole I'd made, but you can't have expected I'd stop and mend it, surely. As it was, it took me all my time to crawl through the hole.

Then I sat and waited on the grass verge. I got out a cigarette but couldn't light it in the wind. What had been blustering at The Beeches was a half gale there.

In all directions I could see nothing but darkness. The sweat I'd worked up was now helping the wind on its way to my tender skin, and it soon became obvious that I couldn't sit there and wait. I stood up. As it was dark I'd got no line of reference, so it was difficult to stand vertical. Then I started moving, downhill because I couldn't have done otherwise.

I could barely see the road. The rain was steadily soaking through my suit and running down into my eyes, and very soon I found myself walking in a limping, crab-like way, in order to keep the wind from my face. There was almost complete darkness, just the tarmac surface faintly grey ahead of me, and here and there the low, curved parapet of a bridge, where I could hear water rushing beneath the road. No trees, at any rate none I saw. Where there were boundaries to the fields, they were stone walls. I don't know what sort of stone, except that it was hard. I walked into it several times.

But there was no traffic.

There comes a time when movement seems apparently to have ceased. All that existed for me was that grey area in front of my feet, never becoming absorbed by my pro-gress. I did not dare to stop; I would never have got going again. At one point I thought: God, a man could die out here. I could feel my body temperature gradually sliding away. They said you dozed, exposure cases, dozed away gently into eternal darkness. I walked in my sleep, numbed and confused, concentrating on the complex business of getting one foot to move in front of the other.

I became aware that a line of stonework on my left was becoming visible. Shadows moved sideways in the screen of rain, consolidated, and became light. Then I saw my own shadow go streaking ahead of me on the tarmac. I turned. Headlights were bearing down on me.

There is no recognized way of stopping a speeding vehicle at night. I did not dare stand aside, or he might have driven past. I faced him, raised my arms, and I think I shouted. The tyres screamed. It reared up in front of me. Somehow, blinded by the headlamps, I fumbled round to the cab door, but I couldn't manage the step. It was some huge vehicle with a high cab. He got down in the rain.

'An accident,' I mumbled.

'Christ, mate,' he said.

He got me in there and slammed the doors. It was hot inside, oh Lord how wonderfully hot! I sat in sodden exhaustion and looked at the streaming window.

'Here,' he said. I looked at him. A fat chap with a moustache and the top off a thermos in his hand. It steamed. It was coffee. Sweet and strong.

'Light me a fag?' I asked.

He gave me one of his own. I drew it in, gasped it out.

'Walked for miles,' I told him.

'Pretty quiet here.' He paused. 'I didn't see anything.'

'Went through the fence,' I explained.

'Why didn't you phone?'

'I didn't see a box.'

'There's one a mile back. No lights in it, though.' He thought about it. 'Vandals, I suppose.'

I said a quiet prayer for vandals, wherever they might be.

'All right now?' he asked.

I said I was fine. The inside of the screen was steaming up when he got into gear and let out the clutch. I think I went to sleep.

He nudged life into me. My first realization was of the pain in my left hand. I looked at it. There was no blood, but things were pointing in unconventional directions.

He said: 'This do you?'

This was a low, softly-lit building down a short drive.

'What is it?'

'Hospital,' he explained. 'You'll need some looking at. You can do some phoning from there.'

It didn't seem a bad idea. He got me down on to the ground. 'Help you in there,' he said. 'Nonsense,' I protested, and promptly went down on my hands and knees. So he helped me in there, into the comfortable lobby smelling faintly of ether and sterilized nurses. I turned to thank him, but he had gone.

It may have been a maternity hospital, for all I could tell. There was a grey-haired nurse behind the reception desk. She looked at me and reached for the phone, said a few quick words, then came round to help me into a chair.

'An accident,' I explained.

'So I see.' She did not approve of accidents.

Then somebody in a white jacket was taking my pulse and two others were helping me along a corridor, through a door, and on to an examination table.

'Better get your clothes off.'

'I'll need them.'

'Not tonight.'

'Tonight,' I said.

He smiled. 'You can have them back. And dry.'

I let them take my clothes away. The right hand jacket pocket was torn away, the one where I always keep my change. I said: 'A sec.' They paused. 'My wallet.' They looked as though I'd accused them of something. 'Thought of something,' I explained, and they relaxed. It was just as I'd suddenly remembered. I'd spent my last three quid on petrol for that batting up and down the M6.

They took them away to be dried.

The man said it would have to come off. It turned out to be a joke. He'd shot my hand full of something and it was beautifully numb. Only one finger was broken, number three, and my middle finger was dislocated.

'Lucky, really,' he said, grinning.

I agreed how lucky it was.

'This didn't come from any car accident.'

'No. It happened in a car, though.'

'I ought to phone the police.'

'A gun butt,' I told him. 'Nothing I can't handle.'

He put a plaster and bandages on it until it was heavier than the rest of my arm. He made a neat job of everything, all the cuts and abrasions.

'Where's my clothes?' I said.

'You ought to stay the night.'

'Business to attend to,' I told him.

He shrugged and went to get my clothes. They'd tumble-dried them, and some kind lady in the far reaches had stitched on the pocket again. But too late to save my small change.

He helped me dress. 'Thanks a lot,' I said. 'Send me a bill, will you. I'm right out of cash.'

'On the house,' he said cheerfully. 'Any time. Come again, it's been a pleasant change.'

He left me in the lobby. I sat down for a minute because my legs seemed to prefer it. Then I asked the old dear in reception if I could use her phone.

'What was it you wanted?'

'A taxi.'

'You're not to do any driving,' she said warningly.

I promised not to do any driving. Certainly not a taxi.

'And you mustn't think of going to work tomorrow.'

I said I wouldn't give it a thought. Tonight for me.

So she rang her nephew or some such relation and asked him to come round. I sat in the lobby and waited. The clock over the dear lady's head said it was ten to eleven.

So all right—I was beginning to worry Finn. Investigating his car, tipping Freer about Busoni—if he'd realized. He'd be annoyed. Then why hadn't he had me killed? Was there still something I could do for him better alive than dead?

Though of course, it could have been a little private party of Troy's, the dear exuberant boy keeping his eye in. After all, he *had* been bored, and I couldn't offer him a game of chess.

My driver was a cheerful little wiry individual, who came bursting in and said, 'somebody want driving home?' as though the lobby was full of us.

'You know The Beeches?' I asked.

'No. Where is it?'

'About twenty miles from Shrewsbury.'

'Man,' he said, 'you're in Merioneth.'

I sighed. 'So I'm in Merioneth. Will you take me?'

He looked doubtful. I didn't exude any aura of wealth.

'Pick up my Porsche there,' I said.

'It'll cost.' He cocked his head. 'Twenty-five quid?'

'Right.' What else could I have said?

I sat in the front with him because I hoped he'd keep me awake. Through the drooping night I heard all about his wife's difficulty with her brother, who was a policeman. I agreed you can't easily live that down.

'You want to stop for a coffee?' he said.

I wanted, I think, more than anything to stop for a coffee, and one of those plates of everything that'll fry that they have at transport cafés, but I was right out of the necessary. I said so.

'My treat,' said my friend, who didn't seem to be worrying about his twenty-five quid.

Which made it a little difficult, and it looked like I'd have to make do with a bacon sandwich, only I must have been salivating or something because he grinned and said go ahead. It is difficult to eat chips and everything with one hand. I managed quite well, thank you very much.

Then we drove on. The stuff they'd pumped into me was working off by now. I had my left hand on my knee, where I could watch it throbbing.

'This is Shrewsbury,' he told me, seeing I was concentrating hard on not noticing the pain.

'Take the by-pass. Turn right for Much Wenlock at one of the islands. I can't remember which.'

It was about two when we reached The Beeches. I told him to drive round to the car park. 'I'll have to get you the money.' But I wasn't sure how or where. I got him to park just inside, and walked on from there. It had stopped raining. The floodlights were doing a good job, and I could see the Rover parked a little to one side of the Porsche. Troy was standing with his back to me, contemplating my car, his feet slightly straddled. I moved towards him with the confident stride of a man about to collect his car. I knew that stance of his.

He swung round, on the ball of his right foot, practising his right-handed draw this time. His left leg was splayed out, his left arm swung back. My own left arm was useless, and my right fist wouldn't have reached him. But my right foot did. The muzzle came up to my eyes as I contacted. He'd got his legs spread and I got him clear in the crotch. His mouth

came open to howl and the gun fell from his hand. I kept
going on in, and scooped up the gun in my right before it
hit the tarmac. This one wasn't plastic. I lashed the barrel
back-handed across his mouth in time to cut the howl down
to a hiss. He swayed, half bent, teeth showing through the
gap in his upper lip, and fell down on one knee.

The safety catch was off. I slid it on, because they can
be dangerous things, guns. Then I slid it off again because
I'd heard the soft snick of a car's door being opened carefully. I turned. The Rover's door was open. A large man was
coming at me fast with the hard light behind him, pre-
ceded by a smell of aniseed. There was a shape in his hand,
so I fired. Not that I expected to hit anything, but I think
I got his knee cap and he went down writhing and screaming. Then it died to a whimper.

I turned back to Troy, who was getting the breath back
into his lungs. I said: 'Get your friend into the car. And
don't try to be clever. I'm feeling nervous.'

He got his friend into the Rover. Blood was dripping
from his mouth. He shut the door and turned back to me.
His face was blank and a greenish colour.

'Reach inside your breast pocket,' I told him. 'Very
gently. No tricks.'

'There's nothing in there,' he managed to say.

'Your wallet.'

He stared. He reached, and produced his wallet.

'Six fivers,' I said.

His eyebrows shot up. 'It's armed robbery.'

'So it is. Six fivers.'

He got out six fivers. I told him to start walking, and
we went over to the taxi.

I said: 'Hand 'em over.'

My driver hadn't missed a thing. He took the money.
He wasn't too shaken to count it. 'There's thirty here.'

c.\

'I owe you for a meal. And a tip. Take my advice and get out of here.'

He grinned. 'Better than the tele it's been.'

We went back to my car. I stood back, and handed the keys to Troy.

'Open the door, wind down the window, and get in.'

I was hoping to give him the impression I was a dead shot with a gun, expecting to be able to pick him off through the window. But I've hardly ever handled one, and there's not many people can hit a barn at twenty paces, if you want to know the truth. I stood to one side, so's not to be in his line if he thought of running me down.

'Start the engine.'

He started it. Nothing else happened, only the gentle clitter of the cold tappets. Of course, they wouldn't have been so stupid as to booby-trap it, but I'd been watching some tele too. I got him out of there. Any second, somebody was going to come running, and I wanted to get away.

I got in, and only then realized I wasn't going to be able to work the gear shift with my left hand. Dave Mallin can be awful slow. I got out again.

All this time Troy had been moving as though his brain had gone sour. Perhaps he wasn't feeling so good.

'Inside again,' I told him.

'Eh?'

'We're going for a run. Get behind the wheel.'

By that time I'm certain he'd realized I wouldn't fire the thing. But he knew I'd hit him with it again if he gave me half an excuse. Troy might have been good at handing it out, but taking it didn't improve his enthusiasm at all. All he did was open his mouth to make a protest, then he got in. Three people were coming down the entrance steps. I slid into the passenger seat.

Perhaps Troy was one hell of a driver in an automatic,

but with a gear box to handle he was murder. I suffered.
I'm not sure which was the greater pain, my left hand or
his driving.

'Birmingham,' I said. 'And use the clutch, you big oaf.
The clutch!'

After ten miles he was getting used to it. All the way
there he snuffled, but I hadn't got any tissues for him. I
didn't speak to him in case I blunted his concentration.
It was very late when I guided him into the crescent where
I live, and got him to climb out. I locked it up.

'Right,' I said. 'Off.'

'But how'd I get back?' he whined.

'Walk!' I felt like snarling, so I snarled. 'Bloody walk,
for all I care.' I turned away. 'Here.' I turned back and
thrust the gun at him. 'Take this thing with you.'

I left him standing in the street with the gun in his
hand at three twenty-two in the morning, and he didn't
send one shot after me.

It occurred to me that some time in the day I should
have rung Elsa. Come to think of it, I should have rung
my brother too. I dragged myself up the steps into the hall
and decided that the morning would be a good time to
start.

Beside the phone in the hall there were two messages
for me. 'Mrs Forbes rang—7.30.' That was Elsa. And:
'Mrs Forbes rang—11.0.' So I'd have to call her, however
late it was. Only this was a pay phone, and I was out of
change. I got up to my dump and hunted for change, but
there was nothing the right shape. I went down again and
asked exchange to see if Mrs Forbes would accept the call.
Mallin this end. You remember, the chap you're due to
marry tomorrow.

'David!' she said. 'Where have you *been*?'

I was tired. 'Touring Wales.'

'I've been waiting all day for you to call, and you haven't. Now you're being funny.'

'I didn't see much of it.' Silence. 'Wales. It was dark.' I could hear she was still breathing. 'Elsa, I'm sorry love. Really. But things happened, and I just haven't been able to get in touch.'

'David, you've got your silly, formal voice on.'

'I'm very tired.' And in pain, and not used to handling a phone at my right ear. 'Did I wake you up?'

'As though I could sleep. Did you ring your brother?'

'There's really no point...'

'But you said you would. You promised.'

Had I? 'He'll be here tomorrow.'

'Today, you mean. It's Thursday now.'

'Yes. He'll be here. There's no question about it.' A pause while I waited for her to say something. As she didn't: 'Is there?'

'I wish you'd check.'

'*Now?*'

'Yes, now.'

'Do you realize the time?'

'Only too well,' she said. 'I've been watching the clock for the past twelve hours.'

'All right,' I said. 'All right Elsa, I'll call him.'

'And ring me back?'

'Of course.'

I hung up and took a deep breath. Ted was in London. It was still half past three in London. I asked exchange to get me the number and see whether Mr Mallin would accept the call. I wouldn't have been surprised if he'd told her to drop dead. But he came on.

'David? What the hell's the matter?'

'Nothing Ted. Just checking things are O.K.'

'What's the matter with you, Dave?' he asked. 'You're

as nervous as a sixteen-year-old virgin.'

'Just checking.'

'We'll be on the eight-seven, get into the hotel about ten-thirty in the morning. *This* morning. Suit you?'

'Yes. Fine.'

'I'll come over and we'll have a natter. The facts of life. Marjorie said I can't let you go in blind.'

Good old Ted. Wake him at three-thirty, and all he thinks about is sex. 'I may not be here.'

'Elsa's?' Ted approved of Elsa.

'I'm on a case.'

'A case? Now?'

'It happens.' I let him absorb it. 'Listen Ted, if we don't get together...'

'Of course we'll get together.'

'If we don't, I've got a taxi picking you up about half past nine, Friday morning.'

'Dave, I can get my own taxi.'

'Then get your own bloody taxi.'

I thought he'd hung up. Then, gently: 'Anything I can help with?'

'Sorry Ted. No. I'm just a bit rough. We'll get together. I'll call the hotel.'

I rang off. Got the exchange. Asked them to find out if Mrs Forbes would... You know the routine.

'It's quite all right, Elsa. You can sleep sound.'

'David, what did you mean about Wales?'

'I'll tell you when I see you, eh?'

'Tomorrow? I mean—today?'

'If I can.

'If you *can*?'

'You see, I'm on this case...'

Nobody said they loved anybody. Once more I'd got a dead phone in my hand.

I didn't trouble exchange again, as I had a fair idea that Mrs Forbes would not be inclined to accept the call.

I didn't have one kind thought about Carter Finn in the ten minutes it took me to get into bed and asleep.

CHAPTER EIGHT

I got about five hours' sleep, then went across the way for breakfast and to split a fiver from my reserve. On the way back I phoned Freer.

'How'd it go?'

'A wash-out,' he said. 'He's a fast mover, this Finn. It'd gone.'

'The intervening walls were knocked down, were they?'

'Yes. It was a good guess.'

'How'd he explain it?'

'Said that by using the end doors they could get six cars in, where they'd only got four before.'

'He's clever, ain't he?' I said enquiringly.

'He's clever. But there's one thing—they had to dump it. We picked it up with only four crates missing.'

'Not quite a complete loss, then?'

He conceded the point. 'But I'm not sure you'll be popular round there.'

I told him I already wasn't.

'So I'd keep away, if I were you.'

'He owes me a drink.'

'How come?'

'He's got four crates out of it.'

Freer thought that was amusing. I don't know why. He said goodbye and see me again sometime.

Ring Elsa? No—call in on the way. Much better. Then she'd actually see me on my knees. I could tell her I was on a job I could drop any second; was just aching to drop any second.

I went back up and got things ready. I dug out the snazzy bit of suiting I'd had built for the wedding, a bit of flare on the slacks, deep vents to the jacket. Hardly me, but Elsa had helped me choose it. I laid it ready with the shirt I was glad I was going to be behind, polished the shoes with some difficulty, put out socks and tie and underwear. All ready, you understand, in case there was going to be one of those rushed jobs at the end. My case was all packed and weighed and the label stuck on. I was free to go out and do some work.

I'd had time to do some thinking about my left hand, apart from the pain I mean. He'd put a pad of plaster in the palm, to stop me bending the fingers, and with a pen-knife I gouged out a hollow that I hoped would fit the gear-change lever. I went down and tried it, and it worked. The impression was of operating things by remote control, but I missed only one change all the way into Shropshire.

I planned to drop into Elsa's first, then my nerve failed and I drove straight on to Crowshaw's. As it turned out it was just as well, otherwise I'd have missed the blackeye.

This time Drover was in the yard. He was now in his sixties, looking somewhat grizzled and stockier, but with the same bright twinkle in his eye. I made myself known, and the old devil actually remembered me.

'You drove for Mr Crowshaw,' he said.

Sharp, he was. Those eyes missed nothing.

'Mr Crowshaw's down in the village,' he told me.

And he'd obviously taken the Land Rover. 'That thing out of order, then?' I asked. I meant the Jag.

He laughed. 'It runs. But the body's about falling off. Mr Crowshaw's always hitting gateposts.'

We talked about the weather, and laughed about those terrible searches in the mud.

'Did you get many sightseers?' I asked. 'After the trial.'

'We did that. But Mr Crowshaw said keep 'em off. Every last one of them.'

'Which was after he'd bought it?'

'He told me that before.'

I could see the Land Rover buzzing up the drive. 'And you were already taking orders from him?'

'He said he was buying the place.'

Crowshaw drove into the yard. He missed the gatepost. When he got down I could see he was still wearing the same clothes. He nodded to Drover and said I might as well come in. With some reluctance. I followed him.

'You're soon back,' he said.

'Things develop.'

'I can't say I'm really surprised to see you.'

The dogs nuzzled their way in from what I knew was the kitchen and he absently ran his hand around their ears. 'Sit down. If you're not in a hurry.'

'No hurry.' I sat down. The setter brought his ears to me. 'Why did you expect me?'

He shrugged. Something had happened to him. There was a firmer line to his shoulders and his eyes were more level, if that was possible. 'You'll have spotted a few points, and you've had time to think them over.'

'Nothing that would help the widow, though,' I said.

'The widow?' He gave a small smile. 'Are we still talking about Myra Gaines?'

'Mrs Gaines—it's Finn now—wasn't my client.'

'Of course not.' He turned away from me and surveyed his domain through the long, low window. 'Young Hutchinson.'

'He was here?'

'As you very well know.'

'But you didn't mention it,' I probed.

'Why should I? You wanted the background to the case, and I gave it you. But Paul Hutchinson's got nothing to do with that case.'

'Had,' I corrected. 'In the past. He's dead.'

I hadn't planned it as a shock remark, so I wasn't disappointed. He merely inclined his head. 'That young chap?'

'An accident.'

'Ah ... yes.' He shook it off.

'But his father—'

'But you say it helped,' he cut in. 'What I told you.'

Paul must have come to see Crowshaw about his father, yet Crowshaw chose to ignore it.

'It was very helpful. I'd been wondering how Myra Gaines could have found herself marrying somebody like Carter Finn.'

'*That* Finn?' Crowshaw was startled. He'd have known Finn well enough.

'That one. But now I understand it. You gave me a very clear picture of her. Demanded attention. She still does. She needed a man who would look at her and see her, and be prepared to be demonstrative about it. Finn does that. She's moving in surroundings where she can act the part to her heart's content, and there's always Finn there to surround her with a warning screen. And he's the type to enforce it. She loves it. You can see her basking in it.'

'Yes, she would,' he said. He was eyeing me consideringly, wondering how I'd been put off so easily.

'There was an incident recently,' I told him. 'Somebody gave her a present. Nothing personal about it, but she had to flaunt it under Finn's nose, and he blew up. I reckon he hasn't seen the last of that brooch.'

'Well ... I'm glad I helped.'

'Yes,' I said. 'It's a pity you're not doing so now.'

'You're not really allowing me to say much.'

'Then I'll sit back.' I sat back. 'And you can tell me all about young Hutchinson.'

He at last took the seat opposite me. 'Paul Hutchinson came to see me. He wanted to discuss his father.'

'It was all he could do. Who else could he go to? Did he show you his father's letter?'

'He did.' Crowshaw knotted his hands together. 'I had to listen to the full story. It was most distressing.'

'It would be,' I sympathized. 'I take it you explained why you had him dismissed.'

'I didn't have him dismissed,' he said sharply. 'I merely put in a report.'

'Which wasn't very helpful to Hutchinson senior?'

'I could only tell the truth.'

'That he'd missed the gun? I'd have expected that to attract a reprimand, at the most.'

He sighed at my ignorance. 'It was not part of my duties to deicide what was to be done with him. Besides, there were other things. He wasn't exactly a man we could be proud of.' He hesitated. 'Other considerations, too.'

I'd been wondering when we'd come to the other considerations. 'Which I wouldn't know?' I waited. Nothing happened. 'And which you're not prepared to discuss?'

'I was merely trying to decide how best to put it. You'll recall that there was a considerable amount of publicity...'

'Damn it all, he never stood a chance—'

'But you're wrong. Behind the scenes, I can tell you now, there was a great deal of agitation from the Home Secretary. As you say, the psychological impact of that second gun being found in such a blaze of publicity was very

adverse to Gaines's chance of acquittal. It was almost impossible to swear-in an unbiased jury. It came to the point
where the Home Secretary nearly recommended a pardon,
simply because he felt that the trial might not have been fair.'
    'But he didn't.'
    'Simply because Gaines was so obviously guilty. His guilt
was never in doubt, only the evidence. But you can imagine
that there were a number of very warm communications
from the Home Office.' He gave a sour smile. 'And all this,
you understand, because that gun was missed on the first
search.'
    I could imagine the rumblings of fury in the high corri-
dors. Somebody had to pay. 'But surely you read that
suicide letter. He did his best.'
    'Not good enough.'
    'Oh, come on. This was a letter he was writing to his son,
just before he died. The one thing he wanted to get across
was that he'd searched that blasted cow byre, and searched
it well.'
    Crowshaw moved his hand impatiently and looked be-
yond my right ear. 'He'd got an obsession.'
    'It followed him all his life. This thing.'

    I jumped to my feet. 'If you can't argue, come outside
a minute.'
    'We can talk in here,' he said stubbornly.
    'Come outside. I want to show you something.'
    He got to his feet reluctantly. 'I don't see the point.'
    'You will.'
    I got him out into the yard and over to the cow byre.
Drover and the pick-up were gone. We stood where the
sliding doors were still four feet open, where Andy Paterson's life had ended.
    'Look in there,' I said. 'Go on, have a good look.'

'I'm not sure I like your tone.'

'Never mind my tone. Just look how dark it is. D'you think it was less dark the day Hutchinson searched it?'

'One's eyes get used to it.'

'All right. Have your eyes got used to it enough to see the straw on the floor? There was straw then. Fresh straw—hay—whatever it was. Much like now. Agreed?'

I was determined to get an admission out of him. Just one. 'Yes,' he said. 'I suppose it would have been.'

'And in his letter Hutchinson said he found three empty shell cases. Was that true?'

'True enough.'

'Brass shell cases,' I said angrily. 'Darned near the colour of straw. Yet in that light, in straw and mud and manure, he found three shell cases for you. And you say he didn't search it well! You've got the utter nerve to stand there and say he didn't do a good job.'

He looked into the murky vastness of its interior. His voice was low. 'And yet he missed the gun.'

'The second search dug it out of here,' I agreed. 'But that doesn't mean it was here for Hutchinson to miss, the first time.'

'You don't know what you're saying.'

'Then why didn't you trace it back?' I demanded.

'There seemed no point—'

'No point! Of course there was a bloody point. You didn't trace it because you already knew damn well where it'd come from, that's why. Hutchinson didn't miss it, because it wasn't there to be missed. And it wasn't there, because you put it there yourself after the first search.'

He gave one bark of impatience, whirled on his heel, and marched back into the house, with me following slowly behind. I paused in the entrance to his living-room, one hand on the door frame, and watched him. He was filling a pipe with short, angry jabs of his forefinger.

'Did he realize?' I asked.

'Who? Realize what?'

'Did Paul Hutchinson realize you'd planted it?'

He lifted his head angrily. 'I haven't admitted—'

'You don't have to. It's obvious. That first search gave you nothing. But you'd done some theorizing. Take a known set of facts, put them together, come up with a logical conclusion. You'd concluded there had to be a second gun.'

'I was right. Right,' he claimed angrily.

'And I suppose no other combination of facts would fit, would it?' I marched across the room. He turned away from me impatiently, and broke two matches getting his pipe going. 'So you had to do your big detective act,' I said. 'It didn't occur to you that the failure might be yours. You couldn't imagine anything else that'd fit the facts. It *had* to be a second gun. Maybe it was your imagination that wasn't too good. But no—oh no—you had to shout your claims—stick your chin out, all confidence...'

He interrupted sharply. 'They'd set me up. It was a gamble. I was willing to take it, but they threw everything at me. Crowshaw said this, Crowshaw promised that. Oh yes, it's easy to criticize now, but I was in the middle of it. I had to produce that gun, or else...'

'Your nerve went.'

He looked sad. 'My faith, rather. The odds were too high, and I couldn't sustain it. It's not a pleasant thing to face. There was just the chance that the second search wouldn't bring it to light, and my stomach turned over at the thought.'

'So you decided to make sure it would?'

He prodded himself into self-justification. 'I wasn't going to be caught on their political roundabout. Not me. Whatever happened, they weren't going to pitch it at me.'

'So you threw in the second gun,' I persisted.

He made a pitiful gesture with his pipe, bringing it up to his mouth though it was cold, then looking down at it with a frown because it had gone out. Even the pipe was against him.

'What's the point in denying it now?' he asked wearily. 'But don't imagine the getting of it was easy. I had only a few days to work in. We'd had the first search, and I couldn't get it locally, of course, or trust anybody else. So I drove down to London. There's connections I've got. I'm not proud of this, you understand. But I got what I wanted. It had to be the same calibre.'

'Of course.'

'And I managed to plant it in time for the second search.'

He sat down slowly. There was silence in the room. I went to his long settle and turned over a magazine. It was his calmness that got me.

'You as good as killed Neville Gaines,' I said gently.

His voice was cold. 'That's not true. I was certain...'

'Your faith in yourself?' I sneered.

'I knew the gun had to be somewhere. The only way my confidence faltered was in believing we would find it. But I knew—'

'From your damned theorizing!'

'It was the only possible solution.'

'No,' I shouted. 'I can give you two or three others. Wild ones, but they're there. You had no *right* to decide that. It was only a theory.'

'He admitted it. In detail.'

'Who the hell did you think you were? Judge and jury? God himself?'

'You're being offensive.'

'And you've got the utter nerve to say I'm offensive!'

He stared at me stubbornly. I just couldn't break through

to him. Was he psychotic or something? All his training and experience as a policeman should have prevented him from even considering such a course.

'As a policeman,' he maintained coldly, 'it was part of my duties to ensure that the ends of justice were not—'

'Ends of justice, hell! You had no right!'

'Kindly control yourself.'

I looked at him in disgust, and banged a cigarette so hard against my plaster cast that it broke in two. The retriever looked in tilted puzzlement at my anger.

'You killed two men. Not just Gaines, but old Hutchinson, too.'

'That is complete nonsense.'

'What's the matter with you? Can't you see anything? In the end that poor devil took his own life, and it all grew from that adverse report. At the time you knew he hadn't missed it. But that didn't stop you. Oh no. Hutchinson had to go.'

'Be quiet!' he said sharply, and caught me in mid-stream. He was actually righteously angry. He stabbed the pipe stem at me. 'I've let you go on. But I'm not going to be called a fool, and an insincere one into the bargain. Why d'you think I chose the cow byre when I wanted somewhere to plant it?'

'Near the body, perhaps.'

He dismissed that idea impatiently. 'Rubbish. I knew there was going to be somebody who'd have to take the blame. Do you imagine I'd do that casually, without a thought? No. I made enquiries. Quietly, of course. I got all the records, everybody who was on that first search. Even you.' He gave a disparaging smile at what he recalled. 'And Hutchinson was an obvious choice. You'll have to take my word for that.'

'Your word!'

'Very well. If you insist, I'll tell you he was no good. Incompetent and lazy. There was a list of complaints as long as your arm. And dishonest with it. We knew he'd covered on at least three burglaries, and there was an armed robbery we weren't happy about. Couldn't prove anything, or he'd have been out on his neck long before. But he was rotten through and through. We were well rid of him, and the opportunity was too good to miss. It had to be the cow byre.'

'And you told him this?' I felt cold. 'Young Paul.'

'Not about the gun. Of course not.'

'About his father.'

'He had to know. It wasn't healthy for him to go on cherishing that absurd idea that his father was some sort of martyr whose life had been ruined by his dismissal. Certainly I told him.'

I wanted to get out of there. I wondered whether Paul had faced it with his sloppy bewilderment. Now, of course, I was beginning to realize why he had come to me. Unable to accept it from Crowshaw, he'd been searching for something, anything, to rescue the image. And on the other side had been the vaguely-menacing figure of Carter Finn. So Paul had called in the big guns. It was a pity this particular gun had only been able to go pop.

'You could have spared him that.'

'I've got no time for sentimental evasion.'

I looked away from him. What the hell was I going to do about it? There'd have to be a report to the Home Secretary, and Myra would find herself right in the middle of it again. Finn wasn't going to like that. That was something I could look forward to with pleasure, anyway.

'I don't know how you've lived with it.'

He made no answer. I turned to him again. He was watching me intently. I'd expected some sort of appeal.

After all these years, let it lie; that sort of thing. But in his eyes there was a deep-felt and unutterable relief.

'You know what I've got to do,' I said.

'I don't know that you need to do anything.'

'You've got no conscience,' I shouted.

Then he lost his temper. He blasted at me. 'Then why the hell d'you think I bought this place?'

My left hand jumped with a spasm of pain. He ignored it.

'The second gun had to be here,' he said wearily. 'Somewhere. All I'd done was put one in to save time.'

'Time,' I breathed. Gaines's time.

'The trial wasn't going to wait. His second gun was here, I knew, somewhere on the farm. All right, so I planted one. It got the trial out of the way. But I was going to make sure the real second one—Gaines's second one—was found. I bought this place. A Chief Inspector with two hundred acres! The mortgage about broke my back. But I had to have it. Then once it was mine, I started in on it. If you want a job doing well, do it yourself. I did it. Yard by yard, working outwards from the house, marking it off. Organized, you understand. Digging down. Because I had to find it. Three years I was at it, every spare day I could get here. Drover must have thought I was mad. I very nearly was, by that time.'

He stopped. I watched him move around restlessly.

'And then?'

He didn't reply at once. He marched over to the Welsh dresser and jerked open a drawer, took from it a bundle wrapped in cloth, and tossed it on to the carved oak table. It unwrapped itself as it fell. I was looking at the rusted remains of a Colt thirty-eight automatic pistol.

I didn't touch it. From behind me he spoke tiredly.

'Gaines's second gun. In the orchard, a few inches under.

Must have worked its way down over the years, or got tramped in.'

'The number?'

'Just decipherable. That was lucky.' He didn't seem inclined to go on. I turned to look at him. He'd waited years for this, dreading it, and now welcoming it. His back was straight, his eyes level. He was filling his pipe calmly.

'So you managed to trace it?' I asked.

He smiled sourly. 'I traced that one. Yes, of course. It had been bought, a number of years before the murder, by Neville Gaines, and quite legally.' Such quiet and dignified triumph. He'd waited ten years to tell somebody that.

'So you were justified. Gaines's other gun.'

'I was relieved.'

He'd been relieved. That made it just fine. And now everybody was happy. I touched it with the tip of my finger.

'How many were fired? Do you know?'

'It's about rusted solid, but I managed to get the magazine out. Three were fired. Then it must have jammed.'

Ten shots, then. We'd found nine bullets, or evidence of nine bullets. That had been mighty close.

'Must have done,' I said. 'But still ... the orchard.'

'I know. We know Paterson didn't go there. I've had time to think about that. Paterson didn't do so, but we can't say Gaines didn't. Maybe in the chase he lost Paterson in the dark, looked for him in the orchard, and couldn't find him. The third shot jammed the gun. Perhaps he let off a shot at a shadow in the orchard and got nothing from this gun, and simply tossed it away. He'd got the other, the one he bought from Lovejoy, and he went on and finished the job with that.'

I felt completely deflated. 'Anybody else seen it?'

He shook his head. 'Myself, and now you.'

'Can I borrow it?' I had to get away and think.

He looked at me bleakly. I wasn't going to let it go. Was that what he'd expected?

'Get a full lab report on it,' I said.

'I suppose it would be as well,' he conceded.

I rolled it up again with one hand, and stood there with it held in front of me. 'Then I'll be off.'

He nodded. What could we say to each other?

The sun had come out. Along the distant road two cars were moving fast. I could just hear them. I turned.

'I suppose you've cleared it now?'

He was in the yard with me, and cocked his head in query.

'The mortgage,' I explained.

'It's clear.'

'Then you're all right, aren't you!'

He didn't admit it. He stood and watched me get into the Porsche and fumble the gear lever into first. The sun went in again as I drove away.

CHAPTER NINE

Freer was in his office. He made an effort to be non-committal. 'Get your drink?' he said.

I rolled the gun on to his desk. He stared at it.

'I'm not going to tell you where I got that,' I told him. 'All I'm asking is a favour.'

'Sit down,' he said, pleasantly enough.

'I don't feel like sitting.'

'Then look out of the window. What d'you want me to do?'

'To start with, don't trouble to trace it back.'

'Very well, if it'll make you happy.'

'Drop it into the lab and let them look at it. Just that. I want to know if it jammed, and why, and how many shots were fired.'

He pursed his lips. 'It'll take a bit of time.'

'I haven't got any time. I'll phone later today.'

'You've got no patience, Mallin, that's your trouble. Nobody's got any patience these days.'

I headed for the door, and got my right hand on to the knob.

'What's the matter with your hand?' he asked.

'Knocked it against a hard object.'

'I told you, he doesn't like you any more.'

I grinned at him. But Carter Finn was going to love me, wasn't he? I was going to bury Neville Gaines several feet deeper under the yard at Pentonville. I turned to go again, but Freer hadn't finished.

'What do I do with it afterwards?' he asked. 'Send it back to Crowshaw?'

I could never stand intelligent policemen. 'Stick a label on it,' I said. 'You might be needing it.'

It was five to one, a reasonable time, I thought, to call on Elsa. If we were still speaking I might persuade a bit of lunch out of her. I rather fancied grilled steak.

The house was quiet outside. I parked and found my way in. It was not quiet inside. I found her weeping in the long lounge, her face covered by her hands.

'Elsa . . .'

She lowered her hands. She had walked into a door. Her left eye was swollen and already changing colour. Somewhere upstairs Doris was on a panic search for repair materials.

'David!' Elsa howled. 'It had to happen now!'

I comforted her a little. Her lips tasted salty.

'What can I do?' she whimpered.

I showed her my hand, which she hadn't noticed before because she was too involved with eyes. 'They'll think I've broken it beating you up,' I said, cheering her a bit.

That did it. Tears stormed down my shirt and her fists hammered on my chest at the thought of it. Then she went silent. She detached her face and looked at me solemnly.

'But David, you're right handed.'

I fell off the settee, laughing. Did I tell you we were on the settee?

'It isn't amusing,' she said pathetically. 'How can I possibly face them like this. How can I go through with it?'

I've mentioned the celebrated Mallin temper. It went. I stood up and told her that if she thought a simple black-eye was going to postpone our wedding, she'd got another think coming. I told her I wasn't going to go through all this preparation and strain again. I told her it was all I

could do to put it off till tomorrow, and if she thought...
And so on.

I'll never understand women. She stared at me as though
I'd brought a stranger in with me, then flung her arms
round me while he was still with us, and gave him such a
warm welcome that it very nearly didn't get put off until
tomorrow. I let it all flow along. You have to make what
you can of the opportunities that present themselves.

Then Doris appeared with some plasters that were no
use at all, and I got a couple of pork sandwiches out of it
in the end, the steak going on Elsa's eye.

'It feels awfully clammy,' she said.

I told her that for some reason I didn't understand it
would be most effective.

'Now you just run off on your silly case,' she said at last,
and off I went, cheerful as the devil until I got in the car
and remembered what I'd still got to do.

When I'd been at Birmingham City Police HQ, Lovejoy
was very well known indeed. For longer than the records
went he had been living in two rooms over a cake shop in
the Stratford Road, and we'd left him undisturbed. We
might have got him on minor charges, but it was more useful to know where we could put our hands on him, and
any crime that threw up a weapon sent us charging round
there to try and dig into his naïve innocence. What he didn't
know about guns was not worth studying up, and the
rumour was that if you wanted to start a war, Lovejoy would
see you went in fully equipped.

On the way through the city I dropped in at the flat to
see if there was any message from my brother. There wasn't,
so I had an attack of nerves and phoned the hotel. Ted was
there.

'We're here now,' he said. 'Relax, Dave.'

'The buttonholes and the corsage for Marjorie,' I said.

'Elsa told me to say they'd be delivered to the hotel.'

'That all right then. Can I come over?'

'I've got to get moving, Ted.'

'If you've got to. Want a word with Marj?'

What can you say to that? 'Of course.'

Ted's wife is a matter-of-fact and unshakeable woman. 'David,' she said, 'how's Elsa?'

'She's got a blackeye.'

It bounced off. 'Has she, poor dear? Never mind. Tell her to wear a thick veil.'

With this thought in reserve, I drove along to Lovejoy's.

You can count yourself lucky if you can park around there, but I found a notch in a side road and walked back. There was a narrow alleyway between a cake shop and a motor cycle emporium next door, and round in the back yard an outside stair up to Lovejoy's place. It wasn't quiet. In the yard next door somebody was blipping a two-stroke. When I got up there, there wasn't anybody at home

I went down into the cake shop and bought a black-currant flan and asked for Lovejoy. The girl said he'd gone.

'This morning,' she said. 'He took a case and went.'

'Any idea where?'

'He doesn't have to tell me.' She tossed her head. 'I don't care if he never comes back.'

I couldn't imagine what might have been between them.

'Did you see him leave?'

'I've got something better to do.'

'I mean ... taxi, was it?'

She sniffed. 'Some big grey car pushed its way in and waited for him.'

I thanked her and stood on the pavement to enjoy my flan and car fumes. Carter Finn was still throwing in obstruction tactics. What'd he got to worry about?

Then I became aware that somebody was operating a car

horn persistently. Amongst the din I detected my name.
'David!'

Karen was out there in the traffic stream because she couldn't get to the kerb, with behind her a string of traffic building up, and fresh horns joining hers. What could I do? Stand and argue about it, until the jam stretched right back to the Rotunda? I got into the Rapier, and she edged away.

'You can't park anywhere,' she complained.

There was a box of paper handkerchiefs in the glove compartment. I used one to get the cream off my fingers, and tossed it out of the window.

'Lucky you spotted me,' I said.

'I'd been round the block three times.'

She was wearing a two-piece in maroon jersey wool. Very smart she looked in it, too. The Rapier slid through the traffic neatly and precisely, heading nowhere in particular.

'Waiting for you to come out,' she said.

She had a small smile, I saw when I glanced sideways, and a quite determined frown.

'Quite a coincidence.'

'Not really. Not at all.' She slipped down to second and nipped into a side street. 'I followed you from your place.'

'Which I suppose you'd been watching for hours?'

'Only one hour.'

'Hoping I'd turn up?'

'What else have I got to do?'

It could be gratifying, the thought that a beautiful young girl should have nothing better to do than park outside my place, just hoping I'd turn up. I had to assume it was Paul who'd told her where it was.

'It's your lucky day,' I said.

'Isn't it? Yours too.'

'I think you'd better let me out, and I'll walk back.'

She had a pleasant laugh. I wondered what the hell she

had in mind.

'I knew you'd be looking for Mr Lovejoy.'

Did she. 'How did you know?'

'If dear Carter wanted him out of the way, then obviously *he* knew you were going to be looking for him.'

Carter Finn was a good guesser. 'And you want me to find him?'

She shrugged. 'It's no good hiring a man, then obstructing him at every turn. Carter's stupid.'

'You should tell him that.'

'I've told him.'

'What'd he say?'

'Told me to drop dead.' She laughed again. This was not the girl who'd tangled with emotions in that living-room.

'Well, I mean,' she said, 'the best thing's obviously to get it cleared, and you won't be finished with it any quicker if you have to search out Mr Lovejoy.'

She was either being very naïve or rather clever.

'You know him, do you?'

'He often comes to the club.' She glanced at me. 'We talk.'

'Then wouldn't it be quicker for you just to tell me what it is you think Lovejoy ought to tell me?'

'Why should you believe me?'

Why indeed? 'Because you have an honest face.'

'Is that what a policeman uses for flattery?' We drove past the Porsche. She kept going, turning back into the main stream. 'Whatever I said, you'd still go to Mr Lovejoy. You'd have to check it.'

'Yes I would.' I watched her concentrating, relaxed but poised. 'If I could find him.'

'He's in Nottingham.'

'A hotel in Cadogan Street. I don't know its name. Troy couldn't remember.'

'Troy told you this?'

'He can't keep anything from me.'

'So you expect me to go chasing off to Nottingham?'

She shrugged. 'You can do what you like about it.'

All she'd wanted was to oppose Finn. Finn hid him away; Karen produced him. But it seemed a lot of trouble for the pleasure of saying, 'so there!' Or it could be a blind, designed to send me in search of a non-existent hotel, which I could not even phone because Troy couldn't remember its name.

'What I'd like to do,' I said, 'is to get out of this car and into mine. Unless you intend to take me to Nottingham yourself.'

She pursed her lips at me, and without apparent thought turned a corner and ran me alongside the Porsche. I got out and turned away.

'Oh David!' I turned back. 'Troy sent you this.'

She was holding in her hand a gent's watch with a gold expanding bracelet.

'He said the watch was a mistake, whatever that means.'

I watched her drive away. The watch said it was ten past four, and it said it over a face that indicated it had cost fifty quid or more. I put it on awkwardly over the stiff mass of my hand, which Karen had carefully ignored, got into the car, and went to look for Lovejoy.

Nottingham is a city I do not know, and Cadogan Street seemed to be somewhere that nobody cared to remember. I was just about to give up when I spotted a patrol car and flagged him down. Yes, he knew Cadogan Street. He was not happy to admit it.

There was one hotel in it. There were also three pubs and seven streetwalkers, to my count, and it was obvious what business the hotel did. It had a narrow entrance in a tall building with filthy curtains, which occupied a

corner where another, even murkier, street led off to obscurity. Round the corner was a public bar. I went inside
the main entrance. There was a dusty lobby with one wall
light, only just hanging on, and a tiny reception desk in
the corner. Nobody was there, but they had one of those
bells you bounce with your palm. This one made a dull
thud. I hit it with my plaster and it rang good and clear.

A man appeared. He had no jacket and wore an apron,
and obviously had been serving in the bar. It was obviously
not an occupation he enjoyed. He grunted.

'Lovejoy,' I said. 'You've got him staying here.'

'Have we?'

'Look in your register,' I suggested. 'Where is it?'

'God knows,' he said, and went back to his bar.

I went behind the desk and found it on a shelf beneath.
There wasn't anybody registered as Lovejoy. But of course
there wouldn't be. But I wasn't going to knock on every
door in the place, so I went out into the street and round
into the public bar. I wasn't looking for a drink, but Lovejoy usually was. He was standing at one end of the bar
with a half of bitter in his hand and a look of complete
misery on his round, pink face.

I don't think Lovejoy has changed at all in the past
twenty years. All he does is buy a new toupee from time to
time, as fashions change. This one had a fringe and curled
under at the back. He looked like a plump and nervous
teenager. He recognized me at once.

'Thank God you've found me, Mr Mallin. I've been
going mad here.'

'You've got a drink. What more d'you want?'

'Who do I know round here? What're you having?'

I had a bitter and he repeated his. It was just like two
old mates getting together, and nobody would have guessed
that the last time we'd met I had given him a very un-

pleasant couple of hours at HQ.

'Not a very good idea, was it?' I asked.

'You mean bringing me here?' He made a disgusted sound, and he had the right sort of lips to do it. 'I said it was daft. What's so terrible about Dave Mallin finding me? That's what I said.'

My change in status was at once apparent. As a sergeant I'd rated mister. I let it go.

'That's what we've got to find out, isn't it?'

'It's that Gaines thing, I suppose. I've already said all there is to say.'

I finished off my drink. 'Then I suggest you say it again. Where's your room?'

'My room!' He raised his eyes in disgust. 'You won't be happy there.'

He took me through a door that came out in the back of the lobby, and we stood back for a big, brash redhead to support her man out into the fresh air.

'You can hear 'em,' said Lovejoy in horror. 'Up and down these bleedin' stairs all night. Giggle, giggle—slamming doors. Must be making a fortune at it.'

I followed him up. The stair carpet was like a sheet of brown paper. 'It makes you wish you could change your sex.'

He looked back at me and leered.

His room had the bare necessities for survival. He'd got a door and a window, a bed and a chair, and a kind of cupboard to put your clothes in, assuming you had any. There was a creamy, perfumy smell that increased when he creaked his weight on the edge of the bed. It had a tatty cover on it, not reaching the edges.

'It gives me the creeps,' he said. 'The thought of getting in that bed again.'

'Then why not shift? You can afford it.'

He looked away. 'It's difficult.' He was scared.

'It's Finn, is it?'

'He said stay here. You know. Said he'd send for me later. How can I move? Go on, ask yourself.'

Carter Finn generated a considerable amount of respect. There had been no difficulty spiriting Lovejoy away. But why? Finn could hardly have known that I'd learn enough from Crowshaw to make me want to see Lovejoy again. All he could assume was that I'd get round to Lovejoy in the normal course of reconstruction.

I offered him a cigarette. 'This Neville Gaines,' I said. 'He came to your place in the Stratford Road?'

'Yes.'

'What did you make of him?'

'One of these cranks. You could see it. Mad eyes.'

'Mad in what way?'

'Never keeping 'em still. You know, all round the room, never looking at me.'

Not necessarily mad, then. More likely interest; Neville Gaines in an environment completely strange to him.

'You sold a gun to a mad customer?'

'It wasn't my worry, what he was going to do with it.'

'No. Anyway, he asked if you could let him have a thirty-eight automatic?'

'Very definite, he was.'

'Loaded?'

'Why'd he want a gun if it wasn't loaded?'

'Ah ... yes.' I could think of an answer or two to that. 'But he definitely said a thirty-eight?'

Lovejoy shrugged. 'Crowshaw asked the same thing. Yes.'

And at the time nobody guessed that Neville Gaines already owned such a gun. So he'd asked for it in those words because that was what his own was called. It was probably inside the lid of the box he kept it in.

'Which you shoved under his nose?'

'Kind of.'

'Then what'd he do?'

'Looked at it.'

'Did he ask you how to use it?'

'Not ask,' he said, 'just sort of sat there looking all lost, and I got to thinking that more than likely he'd blow his own head off if I didn't tell him something.'

'So you offered. What did you show him?'

'Which end the bullet came out, how to operate the chamber, where the safety catch was, what the trigger did.'

'So he was quite an expert when you'd finished with him?'

He thought about that. Outside in the corridor there was the patter of urgent feet.

'I don't think he knew what the hell I was talking about.'

'And he gave you the impression he couldn't re-load?'

'I said I'd show him how to get the magazine out. He said it didn't matter, and just asked how many it'd got in.'

'And you told him seven.'

'I said seven, and he said it'd be enough.'

'Enough?'

It was a strange remark for Neville Gaines. Enough? Hadn't he said something like that to Crowshaw? What was he imagining at the time, the slaughter that it turned out to be?

'And he asked me one or two other little things.'

I didn't remember any other little things in what Crowshaw had told me. 'Such as?'

'How far away it'd kill a man,' he said calmly. 'Where was the best spot to aim for.'

I drew a while on my cigarette. It was dark outside. Thoughts trickled along gently.

'We're talking about the same person, I suppose?'

'They showed him to me. It was him all right.'

Then what could he have meant? 'He told you his name?'

'That was one of the reasons I knew he was potty.'

'And told you who'd sent him?'

'Yes.'

'And who was that?' I asked casually.

'Drover. The chap called Drover at West Lees Farm.'

I went and looked out of the window. The street was drab and poorly lit. A little way along and on the other side a fish and chip shop was open. It reminded me I was hungry.

The chap called Drover at West Lees Farm.

I had always imagined that Gaines would have had great difficulty in getting in touch with such a man as Lovejoy. Yet it had been direct and straightforward. All the same, even though it had been easy, why should he have taken the trouble at all? After all, he already owned a gun himself.

'You know him?' I asked. 'This man Drover.'

'I knew him then. Fairly well.'

'How?'

He looked at his hands. 'You'd better ask him.'

'Maybe I will. And it never struck you as strange that Drover should send you this man—this rank amateur?'

'It did, though. It did.'

'What impression did you get, about what Gaines was going to do?'

'It struck me he was going to have a go at blasting somebody's head off.'

'So maybe you rang Drover, just to see what was going on.'

'How did you guess?' His eyes were big and wide.

Because somehow or other it had got back to Andy Paterson. Myra had said so. That was when Paterson had laughed.

'Lovejoy,' I said, 'they ought to take you out and string you up by the neck until you are very dead. Letting a chap like Gaines walk out of your place with a loaded gun! Damn it, it was ... well, criminal.'

He looked chastened. 'If you say so, Mr Mallin.'

I said: 'You nip across the way for two packets of fish and chips. Plaice for me, if they've got it. While you're away I'll fetch up a couple of pints. Then I'll run you back home.'

His eyes widened.

'Finn?' I said. 'He's not going to worry now. Not now I've seen you, and you've told me so much. You may as well be home.'

'I can't see I've told you anything.'

'No?' I said. 'Can't you?'

CHAPTER TEN

We made it in a little over an hour to Birmingham. It was getting on for eight o'clock. On the way I tried to pump him about his connection with Drover, but I got nowhere. I was becoming quite an expert with the gear change by then.

I dropped him outside his place in the Stratford Road. Lovejoy struggled out, and we rescued his cases.

'Promise me you'll tell Finn,' he said. 'I don't want him thinking I phoned you. I do a lot of work for Finn.'

It made a difference, being out of the force; people told me things. I promised. Lovejoy disappeared down his alley-way, and I went back to my flat.

Messages from Elsa and Ted. Would Mr Mallin phone? Mr Mallin did.

Elsa said: 'I forgot to tell you about the buttonholes.'

'No you didn't,' I assured her. 'It's all laid on. Ted's poised for the off.'

'It's a funny way of putting it.'

'How's the eye?'

'Not as bad as I thought. David, I just dreaded it. But I've got some covering make-up, and it won't really show.'

'Good.' I glanced at my watch. 'I may have time to call in later.'

'Not if you're too busy.'

'I'm not too busy.'

After a while we rang off. I still wasn't used to the phone at my right ear. It was hot.

Ted said that Marjorie said for me to tell Elsa that there was a special make-up for covering blackeyes. I told him she'd already got on to it.

'When're we going to get together?' he asked.

'I just can't say, Ted. But I'll see you tomorrow.'

'If you can stop moving for long enough.'

It was twenty to nine by my nice new watch. I had to cut Ted off or he'd have been on all night.

There was one of those fine, misty rains moving in the air, enough to ruin the visibility. I filled the tank up and set off for Shropshire. It would have cost Paul a fortune, if he'd been alive. When I got there, the floodlights in the car park were cutting cones of light into the mist. The park was decided chilly. I locked the car and looked around. Early yet for the customers; only a few cars there, amongst them Karen's Rapier and the grey Rover. I walked fast for the club entrance. Feeney was not happy to see me.

'Honorary member,' I told him, and he nodded sullenly.

So at least I hadn't been dishonourably discharged. I looked at myself in that tall mirror I mentioned. The suit wasn't evening wear but it was neat enough. The face was looking a bit craggy from Troy's attention; I'd been too concerned about my hand to worry about my looks.

'I heard you had some trouble,' I said, just being chatty.

He raised his eyebrows. Trouble was something Feeney never had. 'It's been very quiet.'

'The police,' I prompted.

'Somebody gave them some duff information.'

I grinned at him. 'People make mistakes.'

'Sometimes once too often.'

I went in. The band was simply playing around, keeping the sound waves moving. I couldn't see anybody I knew in there, so I went to see what it was like in the bar.

It was a little busier. Through the archways I could see

that only one of the tables had its nightdress off, and the croupier was so bored he was using English. Seven people were at the bar. One of them was Karen, perched on a stool and showing all the leg she'd got, and another was Troy, close enough to exude a protective air without actually being with her.

Karen had a wine glass with a pale golden wine in it. She was wearing about two feet of dress in a lemon silky-looking material. There was a necklace of blue stones crackling round her neck and flopping into the cleavage. Karen was flushed and her eyes were bright. There seemed no reason for a flushed young lady with bright eyes to remain un-escorted, so I slid on to the stool next to her and ordered a scotch.

'Well...' she said. 'David Mallin. You do get around.' She giggled. Very slighly tipsy, I decided.

Along the bar behind me a woman laughed with that empty vigour they use when a man tells them a dirty joke. From beyond the curtains the band was playing itself in with a rhumba.

'I've been getting around,' I said. 'But there wasn't any-thing worth all the trouble it took.'

She turned the glass in her fingers, eyeing it at an angle that made her mouth look sulky. 'I got the impression you're an intelligent man,' she said distantly.

'Whatever could have given you that idea?'

'The way you manoeuvred Carter.'

Beyond her, Troy was looking unhappy. 'Five to ten,' I told him, raising my voice and waving my left arm.

He flexed his mouth muscles. The cut wasn't too bad, I saw.

'You knew what had happened,' said Karen, picking it up.

'The brooch? Yes. I guessed.'

'So you used it to get Carter to tell you to go on with the thing.'

'I'm in it for the money.'

She caught the bartender's eye. He was an observant lad; he ignored her. She turned back to me angrily.

'Is she still wearing it?' I asked.

She laughed softly. 'Of course.'

'Risky.'

'He wouldn't dare touch her,' she said fiercely.

'Of course not. Not physically. Close enough for it to be exciting, but not close enough to be painful. But she'll play it wilder and wilder, watching him get more and more mad. Then one day it'll break out into plain, old-fashioned violence.'

She was looking at me with her eyes smoking; warning signals away in the hills. 'He wouldn't dare.'

'Because if he did you'd kill him?'

Then she smiled gently, pleased I suppose at the anticipation. 'I'd have his eyes out.'

Ten o'clock. In twelve hours I was due to be married.

'I'd like to be there,' I said. I meant the eye thing.

'I thought you liked him. Dashing round in your little car, asking questions, getting nowhere on purpose.'

'I don't think he wants me to get nowhere,' I told her. 'Otherwise he wouldn't deliberately put obstacles in my way, knowing I'm going to clamber over them.' I paused, took a sip of whisky. 'With a little help here and there.'

She teased me a bit with her eyes. 'But you didn't get anywhere with Mr Lovejoy.'

'I heard things I hadn't heard before.'

She didn't look at me. A girl has to train herself not to appear too eager. I waited a long time before she said anything, then it was only: 'Tony, let's have another of these things, for God's sake.'

'But they didn't mean much,' I admitted.

'The intelligent David Mallin?' she snapped.

'All I can do is listen. There wasn't anything there.'

'Perhaps you asked the wrong questions.'

'Obviously. What did he tell you that you thought I'd find out? What was important enough to send a young lady thirty miles to wait outside my place on the off-chance I'd call in?'

'It might not seem important to you.'

Tony grimaced as he brought her a fresh glass. 'What?'

'Daddy's state of mind. What he was thinking at the time. Why he was doing all that. You know.'

'Why he was doing what?'

'Oh, you *can* be stupid when you try. All of it.' The wine followed the rest. The glass banged down like a signal.

Down in the gaming room they were working up to French. Trois came out as troy.

'You see,' I explained, 'all he was doing was buying a gun. He was a chap you don't normally associate with guns. It was his first excursion into the underworld, and he was like a traveller in a distant land. Lost. That's the picture I got. A lost and unhappy man—'

'Unhappy man?' she put in sharply.

'I'd hardly imagine he was happy about it; the circumstances under which he was doing it.'

She bit her lip. 'No.'

'So, as I say, a lost and unhappy man.' She'd known about the circumstances, grown up with them. 'Fumbling his way along. Having to be shown how to do this and how to do that.'

'Have you got a cigarette?' she asked.

I had. She drew on it.

'And that's all it meant to you?' she asked in scorn.

I managed to meet her eyes levelly. 'What else is there?'

'What he said about how far away would it kill a man. Where to aim.' She *had* been speaking to Lovejoy.

'If you intend to kill a man, it's best to know that sort of thing.'

Now the scorn was rampant contempt. Her voice had a touch of hoarseness in it, where the emotion touched it.

'You're a very unintelligent man for an enquiry agent,' she cried. 'Anybody else would have realized daddy was lying.'

Troy eased himself on his stool. I glanced round, because the soft buzz of conversation had eased around us.

'So your father was lying. That's very interesting. I never guessed. What was he lying about?'

'Pretending he didn't know which end was which, that he couldn't fire the thing. Of course he could. He'd had one of his own for years.'

So there we were. I was supposed to fall off the stool with shock. This was what it had all been about, this urging me on to seek out Lovejoy. So perhaps if I'd been bright—and if I hadn't already known—I'd have seen that construction in it. But I'm not too bright. She'd had to go to all this trouble getting me to force it out of her.

I don't register shock too well. I compromised by dropping my cigarette. On the way back up I noticed how delicate her feet were. 'Had he?' I said.

It was something she'd secretly cherished for thirteen years, and now its revealing fell flat and empty.

'I knew he'd got it,' she said, pouting. 'He used to take it down into the woods and try it out. I don't think he could hit a tree, but daddy was like that. It was an adventurous toy. He played with it.'

Her voice was low now. Vibrant. There was complete scorn in it, not now for me, but for her father, a grown but immature man who played with his gun in the woods. She was silent. I prompted her gently.

'So he knew very well how to re-load it?'

'Of course he did.'

'So that all this scene of his with Lovejoy was just a bit of background that he was laying-on, just in case the police came into it later, so that he could play that clever trick of his? No, I couldn't re-load! No, I didn't understand it at all!'

'No, no!' she hissed at me fiercely, her teeth tight because she was trying to stop herself from shouting. 'Not for the police. For him. For Paterson.'

It was a pretty piece of work. She wasn't angry at all. She'd got it round to what she'd been intending, which was to show me why her father had gone to Lovejoy. I was not to consider the fact that Neville Gaines had known, all the while, how to re-load the gun, and the inferences that might grow from that. Poor Gaines had been fighting for his life. After the murder he'd been in shock, but all of a sudden he'd realized we'd only found one gun. He'd caught hold of the idea with both hands. It had been a fine act he had put on, but unfortunately he'd convinced Crowshaw that there had to be two guns, and it was now a sad thought that in this way Gaines had precipitated the whirl of publicity that had ultimately condemned him.

'For Paterson,' I agreed. 'The scene with Lovejoy was for Paterson's benefit.'

'Why would daddy want another gun when he already had one? Why would he go to all that absurd trouble to get another one, unless he'd got a special reason? But you can see it.' She stared at me aggressively. 'Can't you? He didn't want to *do* anything. It was just a warning.'

'But he did do something.'

'Yes, later. Later. When the warning had no effect.'

'Yes,' I agreed. 'It makes sense. His attitude tipped off

Lovejoy that it was something out of the ordinary.'

'There you are then,' she said in triumph.

'Yes, there I am.'

But where the hell was I? She had known that her father owned a gun, and perhaps she could expect me to discover the fact. So she had given me a reason for his obtaining a second gun. Valid, was it? Yes, reasonably. Gaines had clearly been rigging the scene as a warning to Paterson. But was that his only reason for searching out a second gun, when he already had one? There could be another reason, which Karen preferred I shouldn't find.

'It's a pity I had to spell it out for you,' she said tartly. 'You're not very sharp.'

'Perhaps I'd have got round to it,' I said. 'Though possibly not to the fact that your father already owned one. They ... we ... didn't ever think either gun was his. The assumption was that he'd gone out and bought two. Two illegal purchases. You must have realized that.'

She'd realized it very well indeed, else why should she now have made such a thing about presenting me with this detail?

'Of course,' she said prettily. 'But I didn't think it mattered. I was only a little girl then.'

But she thought it mattered now. She did not avoid my eyes, and I thought she was simply being naïve. Then I realized it was something else. She was establishing a lack of interest in Carter Finn.

He had come up behind me silently, and there was just a hint of his after-shave in the air. Probably a club owner shaves in the evenings. I turned. I smiled.

An articulated lorry loaded with scotch stood between us.

'Nice to see you around,' he growled. His smile creaked.

'I came for the drink you owe me.'

'Owe you?'

'Four crates,' I reminded him.

A small flood of colour rose above his collar. His eyes were huge. 'I don't get the point.' His gaze enjoyed the wrappings on my left hand. 'But you can have your drink. Tony!'

Tony was there already, hovering, putting another glass in front of Karen.

'Ginger ale,' I said. 'I'm driving.'

'Keeping you busy, is it?' Finn asked nastily.

'I'm running up a lot of expenses.'

No expression marred his face. 'Let me have a list.'

I nodded. Tried the ginger ale. 'I've got a message for you. From Lovejoy.'

He was beside me now. Karen was looking at him with contempt from behind her glass.

'You met him, I hear.'

'He wanted it quite clear that it was me dug him out, and not the other way round.'

To me it seemed that the bar had gone quiet. Troy gently pushed one of his three glasses away, slid down to his feet, and shrugged his shoulders more firmly under the pads.

'All I don't get is how you found him,' Finn said.

I wasn't going to say anything. To show how relaxed I was, I took my glass up again and added a little more to my abstinence. It was because of the glass in one hand and the wrappings on the other that I couldn't prevent what happened.

Karen spoke softly. 'It was me who told him where to go.'

His lips went back. 'You interfering little bitch!' Then his right hand lashed his knuckles across her face.

She swayed back on the stool, made no sound but a surprised whimper, then came forward with her teeth showing and her eyes blazing, and he got the rest of her wine in his face. Then with a whirl she'd got the glass clenched high in her tiny fist and it was on its way down to smash into his eyes. His left hand met her wrist and trapped it. I heard her quick, hissing intake of breath, and his right hand swung back for a blow which could have cut open her face.

But Troy was there. He plucked Finn's poised hand out of the air and held it rigid.

'Easy boss, easy,' he said gently.

Finn turned his face slowly to Troy. I barely heard what he said, but the tone cut like an icy draught.

'Take your hands off me.'

Troy writhed his cut lip into a smile. 'Drop it, Karen,' he said, and she opened her fingers. The glass tinkled down to the floor. A tiny trickle of blood ran from the corner of her mouth. Troy stepped back. Finn shook himself as though he'd just walked through a waterfall.

Then Myra's voice clipped in. 'Carter!' It came from behind us, and I turned to face her.

She had just come through the curtains and was moving rapidly towards us. It was so quiet that you could hear the disturbed air from the hem of her long evening dress. Myra was white. Her lips seemed dark. The brooch sparkled at the breast of her cornflower dress.

'Carter,' she snapped, 'how dare you!'

He told her with a harsh voice. 'I dare because she's had the impertinence to interfere.'

She stood in front of him, shaking. 'I told you never to touch her.'

'I'll kill her if she does it again.'

'You'll do as I say,' she told him, and for one moment I thought her long, delicate fingers were going to fly for his eyes. 'Don't touch her again, Ever.'

And there, in that company, in his own club, Finn could

think of nothing to say. To do, yes, perhaps. I watched his right hand curl into a hard knot of fist. But he did not dare to use it. Not there. I saw the impotent fury rise into his eyes, and he was out of control. All he could do was turn away from it. He did so, then abruptly he whirled back, his fingers clawing.

'And take that thing off!' he snarled.

His fingers closed over the brooch, and jerked. But this time it did not come away. There was a tearing sound and the dress went from neck to waist. He'd got the brooch all right. He'd also got a yard of cornflower material. Then, ridiculously trailing it from his right hand, he stormed off into his office.

Myra was wearing nothing underneath. In the shock of it, she made no attempt to cover herself.

'Mother!' Karen screamed.

She was off her stool like a wild little terrier and heading after Finn. Myra said quite softly, 'No, Karen,' but I don't think it would have stopped her. Troy caught her by both shoulders, shaking his head. For a minute she fought his strength, then she went limp, hanging her head.

Myra clasped what was left of her dress across her naked bosom, and with challenging dignity swept down into the gaming room and across to the private door. When I turned from watching her, Troy was dabbing gently at Karen's lips with one of his paper handkerchiefs and whispering to her.

I finished my ginger ale and headed for the phone booth.

It was half past ten, and Freer had gone home. But he'd left a message that if Mallin phoned he should be put through to the lab.

'Mr Mallin? Mr Freer left a message—'

'I know. What'd you find?'

'It's a Colt thirty-eight, around 1940 manufacture. It's

pretty badly rusted. Three shots fired.'

'And had it jammed?'

'Nothing we can detect. The safety catch was off, and there was no reason it wouldn't go on firing.'

I told him thank you very much, and that it was very interesting.

Everything was quiet in the bar. Presumably Finn would be fuming in his office. Troy wasn't around, and neither was Karen. There was nothing to keep me there, so I left, said good night to Feeney, and climbed into the Porsche.

It was fifteen minutes to West Lees Farm, which made it around eleven when I got there. The night had deteriorated into something dreadful, and I had every reason to expect that any self-respecting farmer would have retired for the night. At any rate, his bailiff should, assuming he'd be up with the dawn, ploughing and scattering and the like.

Drover lived in a cottage half-way up Crowshaw's drive. There was a light in the front window. I got out. He opened the front door with a grating sound. When I got inside I saw the place was old, but not ancient enough to rate ceiling beams.

The front door opened directly into his living-room, which was a big, square room with two small windows and one of those old black ranges in an outer wall. He had a good fire going, and had been watching his television. Just inside the door he had a very fine glass-fronted case containing about a dozen sporting guns. There were two easy chairs in decrepit, beaten leather standing on one of those rugs they used to make with cut strips of cloth.

He'd got one low table in there, with on it a tray with an empty coffee pot and the crumbs of his sandwiches.

'I could make some more coffee,' he suggested.

He wandered through into his kitchen, and I drifted after him. Here it was really old, and tiny. One corner had a built-in square block of brickwork, which was a boiler, if you cared to stoke it up. The sink was low and earthenware, and, like Paul, he had only one tap. He'd got a modern cooker, though, and he'd squeezed a refrigerator into a corner.

'I thought it was time we had a chat,' I said.

He was percolating the coffee. 'A little late.'

'I'm sorry. It was difficult to fit in. I had to chase Lovejoy to Nottingham.'

He didn't react to the name. 'It's taken thirteen years.'

'For somebody to get round to it?'

He was silent for a moment, then he began digging out fresh cups and saucers from his narrow kitchen cupboard.

'We're a quiet lot in the country, Mr Mallin. We notice things, but we don't go running with our mouths open wide. We sit and wait. Sometimes somebody comes along and asks questions. Then we say. If people ask. Do you fancy a piece of cake? Home-made.'

I said I'd like a piece of cake. He was a handy, self-contained man.

We took the tray back into the living-room. He poked a long, thin poker between the bars of the fire, and sparks whipped up the chimney.

I said: 'I asked Lovejoy how he knew you. He said I'd better ask. I came round to do that.'

'He's a delicate lad. He didn't want to land me in any trouble.'

I accepted the coffee. The cake was on a little plate on my right knee. I was going to be in difficulties.

'Would there be trouble?'

Little wrinkles grew in the corners of his eyes. 'Not now. Nothing I'm ashamed of, you could say.'

'So you did know him?'

He moved the low table across, so that I could get both

the cup and the plate on it.

'There was a chap I used to know called Hutchinson.'

'Hutchinson?' I said it in quite a normal voice.

'A policeman from the next village. It's all right to tell you now, because they kind of retired him early. Can't tell you where he's got to, though.'

'I can. He's dead. Six months ago. It was suicide.'

'Ah, yes. He was a rather unstable chap. Anyway...'

They hadn't been very close; there'd been very little regret in those sharp, understanding eyes.

'Anyway,' he said, 'this Hutchinson and me, we'd sort of meet from time to time, and things got a bit friendly. You know. This wasn't his territory but he'd come over, and we'd take a couple of guns out, if we felt like it.'

'Yes.'

'Then one day he said he'd got a chap coming over from Birmingham and he couldn't very well put him up at that station, and could I put him up here.'

'That didn't strike you as strange?'

'Of course it did. But ask no questions and you don't get worried. I said yes. Curious, you see.'

I saw. The cake was fine, the coffee excellent. 'And this was Lovejoy?'

'Lovejoy, yes. About thirty he'd be, then. A queer type, I thought, but he was friendly enough, and chatty. We got on fine. He admired my guns. I've got a Purdy in there he drooled over. Oh, he knew guns, and pistols, and rifles.'

That was Lovejoy. 'And how long did he stay?'

'A couple of nights. He went missing in the evenings. Then he visited again about a year later.'

'And you never found out what was going on?'

'I didn't ask. I didn't want to know. But I saw him and Hutchinson and two more chaps in the Black Swan, and they looked pretty rough types to me.'

Freer had been right, and Crowshaw had been right. Hutchinson had been bent, right enough. The miracle of it was that he hadn't automatically drifted into crime when he was dismissed. Perhaps, out of the force, he was no further use.

'So by that time,' I suggested, 'you had a pretty good idea that Lovejoy's business wasn't legal, and that it involved the sale of weapons.'

He chuckled. 'I knew damn well.'

'So that when Neville Gaines asked you, you knew just where to send him?'

'You make it sound as though Mr Gaines came running, and said where could he get hold of a gun. That's not very likely, is it?'

It hadn't seemed likely at all, and I'd been worrying about it. 'Then tell me what is.'

'You've got to understand about Mr Paterson,' he said. I nodded. 'He'd had the place since his father died. I worked for his father, right from the time I left school, and I admired him. Mr Andy was a different thing altogether. Not interested in farming, you understand.'

'I don't suppose Mr Crowshaw is, either,' I said.

'But he tries, Mr Mallin.' There was a brief flicker of antagonism across his face. I'd upset him. 'He tries.' Then it was gone. 'But young Mr Andy didn't care. As far as he was concerned, the farm didn't exist. He left it to me.'

'Flattering.'

'I like people to show a bit of interest. Look at the place, sometime, appreciate it. But he had fancy ideas. He was a climber.'

'But he didn't climb far.'

'He was busy making connections. Usually female ones.'

There was no doubting, now, the contempt in his voice. Female ones! Drover would have hated them.

'He'd have them up at the house,' he said, 'silly, giggling women, standing with his back to the fire and a glass in his hand like he was squire of the manor or something. I hadn't got any time for that sort of thing.'

'This was before Myra Gaines?' I asked, and then almost laughed at my stupidity.

'There wasn't any after.'

Because this time he'd got himself a female with a quiet and retiring husband who couldn't handle the situation.

'So when Myra Gaines turned up, you knew what the situation was?' I asked.

'Yes.' He looked thoughtful. 'But this time she was a married woman, and there was a husband, and this time he wasn't using a woman for his social thing, she was using him.'

'Using him in what way?'

'To shake her husband up. Mr Gaines was like that, dreamy, couldn't see a hand in front of his face.' He smiled. 'So she threw them together, Mr Andy and Mr Gaines, just for the devil of it.'

'And he didn't bite?'

'There were some funny things said about Mr Gaines at his trial,' Drover said thoughtfully. 'I don't know, it didn't sound like the same man to me. Whatever anybody likes to say, he felt it. Oh yes, it hurt him, and I know it. He was hurt, and damned hard.'

'But nobody else saw it?'

'He was too proud. Just smiled, and said Andy Paterson was a heathen.'

Myra's word. 'And was he?'

'It's a good word.'

'You spoke often together, then?'

He shrugged. 'She'd bring him here, just to watch the two of them together, and Mr Gaines, he wasn't going to

let on he cared a fig. So he'd walk out and leave them to it.
This was all through the summer, you understand. Now
he'd got an interest, Mr Gaines had. He'd see me working
somewhere, in the orchard or haymaking, say, and he'd
walk over and we'd get chatting.

'You admired him?'

'He knew what he wanted. He was a man who knew how
he wanted his life to be, and he went right out for it.'

'And while you were both chatting away, you both knew
your Andy and his Myra were canoodling in the parlour?'

He chuckled. 'Yes, of course. That's another good word.'

'So that your conversation would be slanted towards it?
You'd perhaps mention it. So how did the talk get round to
guns?'

'Well, a kind of joke at first. You know. It was one of
those evenings, the gramophone going in the living-room
and Mr Gaines out smoking on the terrace, and I just
happened to stroll up there. He grinned, kind of, and
pointed his pipe stem at the window, and said it was a pity
it wasn't a gun. I knew what he meant.'

'Did you? What did he mean?'

'He wanted me to pass it back to Mr Andy. Mr Gaines
talking about guns. You know—a gesture.'

A gesture! 'I know.'

'But Mr Andy only laughed.'

'So you did do it?'

'Glad of the chance. I'd have liked to have seen the
smirk wiped off his face.' Drover was looking quite stern.

'So he laughed. And then what happened?'

'They came again. September, I think it was. We'd got
the hay in, anyway. They were at it again, and I strolled
on up.'

'Just happened to.'

He twinkled. 'Yes. And there was Mr Gaines out on the

terrace. So I told him Mr Andy had laughed. He sort of gave a half smile and said couldn't I get him a real gun. You see, more gestures. So I thought, go along with it. See what Mr Andy said then. And I put him on to Mr Lovejoy.'

'And that was the last time you saw Mr Gaines?'

'Yes. I heard what happened, though. Lovejoy phoned me and told me all about it.'

'Which you duly passed on to your Mr Andy?'

'And he laughed again.'

So in the end, gestures not getting anywhere at all, Neville Gaines had stormed up here, and finally wiped that smirk right off Andy Paterson's face.

'I'd have thought,' I said, 'that when it all happened you'd have felt just a little uneasy about the gun. You'd been the one to get it for him. Then your Mr Andy got himself dead. A bit drastic, wasn't it?'

He thought about it, then he spoke slowly, making sure he chose the right words. 'I'll tell you the truth, Mr Mallin. I stood there, and I saw Mr Andy dead, and I thought: that's the end of him. Nothing more. I didn't feel a thing. But conscience? Yes. What got me was that Mr Gaines had done it, and it was me landed him in all that trouble, sort of.'

'So you regretted it?'

'It didn't seem right he should be hanged for somebody like Mr Andy.'

'So that if the opportunity had presented itself, you'd have been glad to do something to help him?'

'I didn't tell any lies. Whatever Mr Crowshaw asked me, I told him the truth.'

I looked at him carefully. He was a man of quiet dignity, a man you could trust. First attract his unswerving loyalty...

I said: 'Correct me if I'm wrong. Stop me any time. I'm

going to take you back to that first day after the murder.
We'd found one gun straightaway. But you were hanging
around with your ear to the ground, and later on there was
talk of two guns. Things were all lined up for the first of
our two big searches, and it occurred to you that you might
help your friend Gaines a little. So *you* searched, before we
did, and you found the other gun. You genuinely believed
it would help him if you hid it. So you took it into the
orchard, and you buried it there. Am I right?'

'Pretty fair right,' he agreed placidly.

'So that you knew, that first big search, and the second
bigger one, that we hadn't got any chance of finding it?
Because we didn't go into the orchard at all, as Paterson
didn't go there, either?'

'All those healthy men,' he said softly, 'in all that terrible
weather. Yes, I knew.'

'I got the pig sty,' I reminded him.

'I remember.' He would.

'And that means,' I said, 'that when the second search
turned up a second gun, you must have known that somebody had put it there to be found.'

'That was obvious.'

'And you said not one blind word?'

He spread his hands. 'What was there to say? That I'd
hidden the other in the orchard? That'd be stupid, now
wouldn't it! I'd done what I could for Mr Gaines. He'd
had two guns, and they'd found two guns. He didn't lose
by it.'

'But they weren't the right two guns.'

'Does it matter?'

'I don't bloody-well know,' I admitted.

We'd exhausted the coffee pot. There wasn't any more
cake. I lit a cigarette. 'But you must have guessed who'd
planted that gun,' I said.

He nodded. 'As soon as Mr Crowshaw said he was buying the place.'

'But you didn't say anything about *that*!'

'Now ... ask yourself.'

'All you could do was watch him search for it?'

Now he was serious. 'I watched him,' he agreed. 'As soon as it'd gone through—the conveyance—he started coming up here. Week-ends. Holidays. He was always up here, and you could see what he was doing. Digging it up, sieving it through. And not finding it. But he went on. You could almost see him breaking up. On and on, month after month. Then year after year. And I could see he wasn't getting much nearer. In the end, it took three years. He'd sorted through near-as-damn-it four acres. I knew he'd get it, that Sunday. I saw him find it. I saw the expression when he got it into his hands.'

There was almost awe in Drover's voice when he finished, something like wonder in his eyes.

'Drover,' I said, 'you're a sadist.'

For the first time he spoke sharply. 'And what could I have done?' he snapped. 'Dug it up and left it where he'd find it sooner? No, that wouldn't do. When he got to it, it'd need to look as though it'd been undisturbed.'

He was right, of course. I cursed Drover for being so perversely right, and so wrong with his rightness.

'Then it all came right in the end,' I assured him. 'Like a fairy story.'

We said good night amicably enough. He stood in his doorway, and my hand was on his little gate. I turned.

'Oh, and one more thing.'

He smiled. 'I thought you'd missed it.'

'Where did you find it?'

'In the cow byre,' he said. 'It was the first place I looked, Mr Andy being dead in the doorway.'

CHAPTER ELEVEN

I turned round in Crowshaw's yard, parked, cut the engine, and got out. Then I went and pounded on his door. It seemed a long time before I heard his voice.

'What is it, Drover? What's the trouble?'

Then he opened the door and saw it was me. He'd got a quilted dressing-gown over his pyjamas, and his hair was standing out in all directions.

'Mallin!' he said. 'What's the meaning of this?'

One of the dogs menaced me with a low growl, and I pushed past him. They recognized me and relaxed. I put Crowshaw's living-room light on and led the way in.

'I've been talking to Lovejoy,' I said.

'Have you got me out of bed to tell me that?' he demanded angrily.

Bed? What was that? I was hours away from mine.

'That and a bit more. You interviewed Lovejoy twice. Maybe more. You had all the time in the world to talk to him, and you never spotted it.'

'Spotted what, for heaven's sake? Make sense, Mallin. You're raving.'

Maybe I was. Tired and depressed and out of patience. I tried to steady myself. I said:

'The way things went between Gaines and Lovejoy. All that business about showing him how to fire the thing. And something you never heard at all. Gaines asked him how far away it would kill a man, and where to aim.'

It stirred something in his eyes. He went and sat down

and prodded the fire. 'I didn't know that. But if I had, I don't see it would have been significant.'

'It would if you followed it through.' I couldn't sit; I had to move around. 'Gaines was rousing Lovejoy's curiosity. He was making a gesture he knew would get back.'

'Get back?' He looked startled. 'Get back where?'

'Here, damn it,' I cried. 'To Paterson.'

'But how could it do that?'

'You never asked Lovejoy who'd sent Gaines to him.'

He suddenly saw what I meant, and he wasn't happy. 'I didn't. Who?'

'Drover, that's who. Your Drover.'

'Impossible.'

'Then ask him. Ask him, when you've got time. Drover put him on to Lovejoy, so Gaines knew the whole thing would get back. Myra said Paterson had told her that her husband had bought a gun, but you never wondered how Paterson knew. If you'd found out, you'd have questioned Drover. But did you? No. You'd have found out some very funny things about Drover.'

'Drover,' he murmured. He seemed dazed.

'Who do you think buried Gaines's gun in the orchard?'

'Oh ... good Lord! Buried? Not Drover?'

'Exactly. Drover. Drover buried that gun. And if you'd got *that* out of him, you'd have found the gun, and you'd have known Gaines owned his own gun, *and* knew how to re-load it, *and* could fire it. And maybe you'd have seen the reason for his ridiculous gesture in going to Lovejoy at all.'

I was watching him crumble in front of me. He'd been proud of his knowledge that his actions had been justified. But now the pride was stripping off, layer by layer. I could have been sorry for him, only I was too busy being sorry for a poor devil called Neville Gaines.

'And what was the reason?' he said softly.

'To send back a warning to Andy Paterson,' I shouted. 'That's what. He couldn't think what else to do. He was near to breaking, and he knew it, so he had to send back signals that he hoped were menacing. Why else would he go out for a second gun, when he already owned one?'

'I didn't know he owned one. Not till years later.'

'Then you should have found out.' I was trying to light a cigarette, but every time my lighter got near it, my hand had to take it out of my mouth for more talking. 'Then maybe we'd have got a true picture of Neville Gaines. Everybody helping him! Drover hiding the gun; Myra saying nothing about him owning one. All very touching. They thought they were helping him. But Christ, they were digging his grave. With the full background—man, don't you see it?—they'd have brought in something like temporary insanity. I don't know. But he wouldn't have hanged. He'd be alive now.'

I let him absorb that. There was a pause long enough for me to get the cigarette going. Then I looked at him. He'd shrunk down into the chair.

'Where,' he whispered, 'did Drover find Gaines's gun?'

I laughed. It sounded terrible. 'In that cow byre of yours. Funny, isn't it! Then you had to go and choose exactly the same place to plant yours.'

'I chose it for a reason,' he said with pathetic dignity.

'Because it was Hutchinson who'd searched it.'

'Deeper than that,' he said eagerly, probing for some vestige of my good will. 'It wasn't a coincidence that I had Hutchinson searching the cow byre. Not by any means. We put the weakest men in the most unlikely places. Hutchinson couldn't be trusted. So we put him in there.'

'Oh fine. That's dandy. So Gaines's gun was found by Drover in the least likely place. I hope that makes you happy. You're damned theorising was way up the creek.'

'Mallin!' He'd had enough.

But I had to shout at somebody or I'd explode. 'There *had* to be two guns. Very clever. But even that was based on a false premise, that Gaines couldn't re-load. He'd got you fooled all ends up. Then you failed to dig deep enough into Lovejoy. You failed to uncover Drover as the connection, you failed to see it all as a gesture. Damn it, man, you failed all along the line.'

He stared down into the depths of his own inadequacy. It was an ugly thing for him to have to face. I was surprised he could speak at all.

'Is that all?' he muttered.

'It's all for now.' I turned away. 'Don't worry, I'll find my own way out.' I got to the door, had it open, then turned back. 'One other thing. Are you listening?' His head came up at last, and he was a poor bewildered old man. Oh, I was enjoying myself. 'That gun, your precious find after three years of relentless toil—it *hadn't* jammed after its three shots. Now you get back to bed and think that one out. And good luck to you.'

Outside in the yard the thin rain pressed gently on my face. I looked up into it. It felt good and clean.

'Good luck to you,' I whispered.

I hoped that Paul Hutchinson would be pleased with me. It was what he'd wanted, wasn't it?

It was twelve-forty. Late or not, I had to call on Elsa. But she'd be asleep by now—her beauty sleep. I drove fast for her place. She'd got beauty to spare.

She was not asleep. There was a light on in the window that I knew belonged to the kitchen, and hearing the car she had the front door open before I reached it. She must have run.

I don't know what I'd expected. She was in a flowered dressing-gown and no make up, and looked so adorable

that I couldn't help smiling. I took her hands and spread
them out and got her under the light.

'Let me have a look at you.'

'Now don't be silly, David,' she said, but she was happy.
Then she touched my face tenderly. 'You should be home
and asleep. You look terrible.'

'Going home,' I promised her, and I let her lead me back
into the kitchen.

She had made herself some tea and was having sandwiches.

'I couldn't rest,' she said. 'I'm like a silly girl.'

'I wouldn't say silly.'

'You can have a sandwich, and there's plenty of tea.'

So I had a sandwich and plenty of tea.

'Promised I'd call,' I said.

'You didn't come all the way from Birmingham for that!'

'A Mallin promise is a promise. But I was quite close.'

A shadow crossed her face. 'That case.'

'Just one item to polish up.' I tried not to look at her.

'But it's after twelve!'

'I know.'

She moved out of the range of my eyes, and I couldn't
see what she was doing. I heard a cupboard door close.
From behind me she spoke quite quietly.

'It must mean a great deal to you.'

'I don't know,' I admitted, watching a tea leaf rotate.
'Something that got started, and I'd like to finish it.'

I turned. She was watching me with frowning attention,
no emotion, no disturbance. This was the Elsa I knew and
loved, the calm one, the practical one.

'Get it done with,' I suggested. 'Out of the way.'

'I know you, David. I know you very well. It's dangerous, isn't it?'

'It could be. I'm not sure.'

'We're very nearly married. I could forbid it.'

I thought about it. 'I'm sorry, Elsa.'

There was a sudden sparkle in her eyes. I was expecting a violent reaction, but she simply sat down opposite me.

'David, you know I'm not going to stand in your way. Not ever. I didn't want you to go into this thing, but you're a stubborn man. Whatever you are I don't want to alter, because I love you because of it—or in spite of it. But David, love, promise me something.'

'Anything.'

'When it's over—when you know it's over—will you phone me? Please. Tell me you're safe.'

I touched her hand. 'I'll do that.'

She smiled. 'There's another sandwich, if you want it.'

But I was full of sandwiches, and there were things to do. I stood up. She came to her feet, still smiling.

'You can kiss me, David,' she said. 'But be careful.'

She was shaking. I kissed her as an uncle might, because anything more would dislocate my whole programme. She didn't come to the door with me. I shut it quietly.

There was no traffic on the road. I drove fast. There was company I yearned to part with, but I had to meet them first.

It was the busiest hour for Carter Finn Enterprises. The car park seemed full. The rain had eased but you could still feel it in the air. I had a little difficulty parking. Then I sat and tried to decide how best to handle it.

Clear through the night I heard a woman scream. It seemed to be close. I scrambled out and looked round. Fifty yards away was standing the grey Rover. A woman was at the offside door. She had it open and was looking down at her feet. As I watched, she fell to her knees on the wet tarmac and she screamed again.

I began to run.

When I was half-way there I saw it was Karen. She had a cape that looked like fur over her shoulders, and she might have been about to get into the car. She heard me coming and turned her startled face towards me, white in the rim of the light, her eyes staring. There was something in her hand.

'Karen!' I shouted.

Then she was on her feet, was stumbling and scrambling, thrust her way clear of the car's door, and ran from me towards the club entrance. I skidded to a halt beside the car.

I knew it was Troy at once, by the plum-coloured dinner jacket. As she'd opened the door he had fallen out on her, and he lay now with his legs still inside. His face was turned up towards me.

I got down on one knee. There didn't seem to be any doubt about it, but I fumbled round for his pulse. His face was purple, the eyes staring and suffused with blood. There was no pulse. Whiteness glittered between his teeth. I thought at first it was froth, but then I realized it was a paper handkerchief. It had become necessary to stop Troy's mouth, so they stuffed it full of tissues. They had continued to stuff them in until he had choked to death.

I thought he would be tidier in the car so I levered him up. Troy had been heavy for his age. The empty box rattled round his feet.

I reached into his waistband, but it wasn't there. Then I knew what Karen had been holding. I set off at a run for the club entrance.

You can't just blast in at full speed, even in emergency. I caught myself in the entrance and steadied to a fast walk. 'Karen come through here?'

Feeney was looking startled. 'A couple of minutes back.'

I ran my hands over my hair and went on through. There

was no disturbance in the atmosphere they were absorbing at the bar, so she hadn't gone through with the gun in her hand. I followed across the gaming floor. They were still faiting their jeux. I went into the hall, and took the stairs two at a time, the hall at a controlled gallop. I knew now where the button was. The door opened silently. I moved inside.

Karen was standing a dozen feet to my left, her cape at her feet. She had on a fine check two-piece in red and gold, nicely set off by the gun in her right hand. Across the room, facing her, was Finn, his right hand in the pocket of his slick grey jacket, and he was laughing at her with that shishing noise of his. There was nothing amusing in what she was calling him, but maybe he reckoned he could afford to laugh, because that hard, bulky shape in the fist in his pocket had to be a gun.

Myra was further across. I didn't have much time to look at Myra, but I got the impression of white, strained features, and a hand to her mouth.

There was going to be a time when Karen ran out of words. Behind me, the door closed with a soft swish. Her voice rose to a crescendo and her hair was a wild cascade over her eyes.

She fired the first shot as I started moving. There was no likelihood that she would hit him. Porcelain exploded and went flying in splinters. She fired again. I was coming in fast. I reckoned he'd allow her three shots. Glass shattered, and in the falling clatter Myra was screaming. Out of the corner of my eye I could see that Finn had his gun out into the open. Karen fired again.

I got her with my right arm round her hips and my right shoulder into her soft young buttocks. At the same time I heard the heavier crash of Finn's weapon, and she seemed to twist in my arms under the impact of it. We

went on across the room, spinning on to our backs and
taking a small table with us, and ended up against the
front of the settee. She was on top of me. Blood dripped
on to my face.

Across the room, Finn was just lining up his forty-five
revolver for a second go at it.

I shouted: 'No! You're too late.'

He shrugged, and slid it into his pocket.

Karen whimpered. I moved from under her. Judging by
the tattered holes in the material, the wound was neatly
through the fleshy part of her right upper forearm. Her
face was puckered and she seemed to be drawing in her
breath in one long and continuous intake.

'Easy now, easy,' I said.

She screamed. My face was close to hers, and I couldn't
take it. I slapped her hard and it cut off short.

Then Myra moved into my circle of vision. She had obviously handed in her resignation as hostess at The Beeches,
and was wearing a pink housecoat over lounging pyjamas.
The legs were pouncing past my face, and I saw where
they were heading. Troy's gun lay on the floor a few feet
away. I scrambled sideways and reached for it, but all I
could get to it was my left hand. It beat hers by a fraction
of a second, but I'd got no grip. For a moment we were
still, she with her delicate hand clamped over my dressing.

'Let her have it,' said Finn sharply.

I let her have it. She came up straight, and from where
I was her face was carved and cold. Finn was watching
her. He had both hands and no gun showing, and there
was still a smile left out of the laughter he'd thrown at
Karen. Myra's gun was steady as a rock and levelled at
his head. He began to walk towards her, his right hand
outstretched.

I heard the click of the firing pin on the empty breech.

He said: 'He did everything in threes. Why d'you think we called him Troy?'

Then he took it from her hand casually, turned, and walked with it to an inlaid table next to the bookcase Karen had blown the front from. I would not have wished to turn my back on Myra. His nerves were doing fine. Mine were in tatters.

Myra sat suddenly on the settee and put her face in her hands. I got to my feet. Karen was sitting whimpering on the floor, her left hand over the wound, and blood running from between her fingers.

'Oops,' I said, and got her up beside her mother.

Finn went to pour himself a drink. He showed Karen the concern that a bullock gives to a wounded bird.

Myra was emerging slowly from her personal shock. She looked at Karen with wild eyes, and only then seemed to realize. I heard her breath hiss in and she gave a moan that might have been a word, but I didn't catch it.

'Brandy,' I said to Finn over my shoulder.

Myra was up like a flash and heading for the bar. Finn was coming away from it with a glass in his hand, and she swept through him as though he wasn't there. He raised his eyebrows at her.

Brandy doesn't help with wounds. But Karen looked as though she needed it, Myra too, and while we're at it, I could have used a shot.

Myra came back with one glass. Karen's blood had ruined the tricky little two-piece, and was doing the same to the settee covers. She gulped down brandy, and choked. We prised her fingers from her arm and got the jacket off her. It was a nice, clean wound.

'Bandages,' I said. 'Something to bathe it with.'

Myra looked at me sightlessly, but she got up and went away.

I said to Finn: 'You ought to ring a doctor.'

'I've got my own doctor.'

'I'm sure you have. Then phone him.'

He looked at me. That gun of his wasn't going to stop me dialling 999 and getting an ambulance there, and he could see it. He nodded and went over to the phone.

'Is it bad?' I said.

'Kind of hot,' Karen whispered. But the pain would come.

I got her stretched out on the settee, just as Myra came back with a roll of bandage and a plastic basin full of steaming, milky liquid smelling of antiseptic.

'Get something to cover her with,' I said.

She went away again. I cleaned the wound. Pain was getting through, and Karen clenched her teeth. The best I could do was put a tight dressing on it and cut down the blood flow. Myra hovered with a lemon-coloured blanket with satin edging. Then we settled her down, the blanket over her, her face ghastly just over the rim of yellow satin.

'Bed,' I said. 'Could we get her to bed?'

'No,' Karen said in a surprisingly strong voice. She gave me a weak smile. She was intending to listen to what Dave Mallin had to say. A lot of good it was going to do her.

On one of the easy chairs Myra was hunched up, hugging herself with her hands tight on her shoulders. I went a walk round the room, Finn's eyes watching me heavily. When I got to the bar I got a brandy for Myra and put it in her hand as I passed her.

'You make a good entrance,' said Finn.

'It wouldn't have helped you.'

'Such a reliable witness?'

'You wouldn't have got away with it. In fact, you're not going to.'

'Self-defence,' he protested.

I laughed. 'You knew the kid couldn't possibly hit you with the thing. You reckoned you'd give her three. In fact, you knew she'd only got three. Oh, it took some nerve, I'll grant you that. But you've got nerve.' I watched him nod. 'So you let her have her three shots, then you'd have got her, clean between the eyes.'

I heard Myra gasp. Finn didn't take his eyes from me, but he made a small, silencing gesture towards her.

'Self-defence,' he claimed again.

I shook my head. 'You certainly hate her.'

'She interferes.'

'Not enough for hatred like that.'

I looked across at Myra. She was caught in a tangled mixture of emotions, because she knew, at once, what was sufficient to goad Finn into such hatred. He loved Myra. Whatever else he might be—aggressive, coarse, tough—he nevertheless loved her, and resented the closeness between the mother and daughter. I could see it there in the eager reaching of Myra's expression, the awareness of what that meant to her. But only a few feet from her, her daughter was lying, in pain now because of him, and she could not forgive him that.

'But she interferes,' he repeated harshly.

I sighed. 'I haven't enjoyed any of this business. Not one minute. I haven't even known who I'm working for and what's been expected of me. There's been some mossy old stones I've had to turn over, and what's been underneath hasn't appealed to me at all. But I've done Paul Hutchinson's job for him. He wanted the truth about his father, and why he was dismissed, and I've cleared all that. So my job's done. It's a pity it had to get so messy on the way.

I smiled around. 'So I'll just say good night.'

It was not conceivable that Finn would simply let me

walk out of there. I'd only moved a yard when the gun
made an appearance again.

'You can't imagine...' he began.

'I can't imagine you ever having one thought,' I agreed.
'It's got to be guns, hasn't it? The answer to everything.
Bang, bang—another problem solved.'

He gestured with it. I was two yards from him.

'But who d'you think you're protecting, Finn? Tell me
that. Yourself? But you've got everything covered, I'm sure.
Troy, out there in the car? Where'll that body be in a
couple of hours? Or the shooting of Karen? I'm sure you'll
fix that, somehow or other. You'll persuade her. You're
great at that. So she'll cover for you—say it was an accident
or something. So what's scaring you, Finn?'

The gun wavered, but only to a point between my eyes.

Myra said hoarsely: 'Let him go, Carter.'

I watched his eyes. He was suddenly uncertain.

'He's worried about Paul Hutchinson,' I told her over
my shoulder. 'There's still the murder of Paul.'

'Murder?' he said.

'I'm the only witness, remember? I can say it was murder.
So all right, you shoot me, and you'll be safe.'

'Me?' he shouted. 'What the hell you mean?'

'Then who else are you protecting? Somebody from here
did it. They watched Paul drive away, then followed in the
Rover.'

'Troy. Troy could've—'

'Oh no. That was not his way. I admit it'd be convenient
—for you. And anybody could say Troy'd not be too keen
on watching Paul and Karen disappearing into the conservatory. But if it'd been Troy, there'd have been no mess-
ing about with cars. One clean shot, that was his mark.
Not Troy, mate.'

'You're not pinning this on me.'

'I agree. I'm not. So why are you waving that gun at me? It couldn't have been a man who killed Paul.'

There was short silence. Finn's eyes moved past my shoulder. 'Sit down,' he said. I didn't move. His face hardened. 'Why couldn't it have been a man?'

'Because whoever killed Paul went on to his place and pinched a letter he'd got. That letter was important, they thought. It was from Paul's father, and Paul had made quite a fuss about what his poppa had said. So it seemed important. Maybe it was, but poor Paul had been giving the wrong impression around here. There's no doubting he wanted to stir something up. But not here. He'd got his sights on a certain ex-copper called Crowshaw. It was all a damned waste, because Paul was killed for nothing. Just for that letter. But the point is that *only* that letter was taken. It was in an envelope. A man wouldn't have done that. He'd have pocketed the lot. But a woman—a woman in evening dress with a dress handbag no bigger than your hand—she'd have taken only the letter, because she wouldn't have had room for any more. So now who're you protecting, Finn? Myra—or Karen?'

I was getting to him. His jaws moved as he chewed on it.

'Well maybe you thought it was Myra,' I said easily. 'But it had to be somebody who knew there was a letter. Up to then, Paul had only said something about where the gun was found. And who'd know he was getting his information from a letter? Who was in the best position to extract information from him? Who was the expert at it? Who else but Karen?'

I had to reckon that his hatred for Karen was strong enough to override his personal considerations. If he let me walk out of there, he knew I'd run for a phone. I looked round. Karen's eyes watched me from over the top edge of the settee. Myra stood still and erect. Two people would have shot me out of hand. I turned back. The third one was smiling gently. One person hated Karen enough.

He tossed the gun, caught it in his palm, made a stiff, ironic bow, and began to move aside.

I went forward towards the door. 'Carter!' Myra screamed, and she started to run towards him. She wanted that gun. I brought my left arm up as hard as I could, and met his face on the way down with its bow.

I don't know what it was like from his end, but I'll never forget what it did to me. Pain shot up my arm like a sword thrust and came out of the top of my head. I'd intended to dive for his gun. So much for intentions! For two seconds there was a blinding whirl in front of my eyes, and when it cleared all I could see was a big round hole a foot from my face. Myra's expression behind it held little hope of my survival.

I was sitting on the floor. Beside me, also sitting, was Carter Finn. The only satisfaction in it was that he was worse than me. They'd never build a nose out of that mess, and his lips were a nasty opening. But Myra needed him now. She needed his help, if I was to be removed, as a dead body.

'Carter, get up,' she said.

He couldn't get up. She turned on him and lashed at him with a bit of expert language, but he only groaned and covered his face. She didn't know what to do.

My head was clearing, though there was nothing but horrible pain below my left elbow.

'He knew,' I said. 'He must have known all along. Else why'd he hate Karen so much? Because Karen had killed Paul, that's why, and all to save her mother from getting pitched back into the Neville Gaines mess.'

Myra's face softened. 'There was no need,' she whispered. Then she backed off, feeling behind her for the edge of a chair. I got myself twisted round, reached my right hand under me, and levered myself up. Gently, oh so gently, because that hammer was cocked and it'd need only a nervous twitch to blow my head off. I moved sideways.

'No need,' I agreed. 'You're right there. It's achieved nothing, because it's all going to come out.' I slid on to a chair beside the telephone. Finn was crawling across the floor. 'Crowshaw is going to reveal all. It'll stink from here to ... to Pentonville.'

She flinched. 'I don't want to hear.'

But she was going to, if it was the last thing I did. 'How Neville Gaines was railroaded to the scaffold,' I went on, relishing the words. 'You'd like to hear that.'

The gun was now resting in her lap. Myra had had about enough. I gave her some more.

'For instance, the two guns. Let's just think about those. There were two guns mentioned at the trial, the one Neville got from Lovejoy, and the one that turned up on the second search.'

Myra muttered: 'I remember.' Karen said nothing. Her eyes were nearly closed. Finn was levering himself into a chair. The front of his shirt wasn't pretty.

'You can forget the gun the second search threw up,' I said. 'It was planted. That's where Crowshaw came in. But it did give the idea, at the time, that Neville had gone out and bought himself two guns.' I glanced at Karen. 'But I now know he'd owned a gun of his own for years.'

Myra fluttered her eyelashes.

'The interesting point,' I went on, 'is that Neville should have gone out and bought himself a second gun, when he already owned one. It wasn't the matter of the number of shots he'd have available. He knew well enough how to re-load. No, there had to be another reason. That was where Karen stepped in, and produced another reason for me to look at. Lovejoy had been talking with Karen, and people who get talked to by Karen have a habit of saying things.' I smiled at her, but got nothing back. 'They say things they shouldn't. And Karen found out there was a direct contact back from Lovejoy to Drover, and then to Andy Paterson.'

Myra was moving her head backwards and forwards in stubborn rejection. But I wasn't going to leave it alone.

'The inference was obvious. It was that Neville wanted the warning to get back to Paterson. Paterson was the one huge stumbling block that'd got to be climbed over.'

Myra spoke softly. 'That's hardly a true picture.'

'Oh, come on,' I scoffed. 'You'd been having it off with this Paterson gigolo...'

She gasped. My tone had been exactly right. 'How dare you!'

'Well, what else?' I demanded. 'Neville had been watching things. He saw that this great oaf of a farmer with his neighing laugh and his slapping of shoulders had got something special for you. He'd seen what you did when Paterson got near you, went all soft and flabby...'

'You're lying,' she snapped.

'It's how it seems to me.'

'Then you haven't looked very far.'

'I can only go by evidence.'

'Andy was a friend.'

I turned my head away in disgust.

'A friend,' she shouted. 'You know that very well. He was attentive, he gave me things that Neville never considered I ... Are you listening?'

I tossed it at her. 'I'm listening.'

'He gave me courtesy and deference and ... and attention. He was a gentleman.'

'He was a heathen.' I might as well have slapped her

with the word—Neville's word.

'You're not to say that,' she whispered.

'But I do, because he was. Andy Paterson was a heathen, and you know it, and you'd got no feelings for him at all.'

She made an angry movement. Karen's voice came over the back of the settee. 'Mother, please!' Karen was trying.

I said quickly: 'You're a woman of sensibilities, Myra. You're emotional and you're intense. You and Andy Paterson! You told Crowshaw you loved him. Nonsense.'

I was Neville again, not believing and not accepting.

'Neville,' I said, 'would never have believed it.'

'But he did,' she claimed, almost pleading.

'Never. You could have thrown Paterson at him till Doomsday, and Neville would simply have ignored it.'

'He believed. Oh yes, he did. In the end.'

'You got him round to it, did you?'

There was a hint of a smile of triumph on her lips. 'Well ... he did go to Mr Lovejoy and buy that gun.'

'Ah yes, Lovejoy's gun. Neville's gesture. Here was Neville Gaines, the artist, the poor lost soul in the wilderness, who couldn't stand up to anything ... here he was, having to consider an unimaginative and boorish clod like Paterson. And he went out and made a gesture! A gesture? Ask yourself. What could he have expected from that? Nothing but one of Paterson's neighing laughs. Don't give me that rubbish. Neville wasn't making gestures to Paterson. Now, was he?'

Finn leaned forward and made a croaking sound.

'It's gone far enough,' said Karen hopelessly.

'No!' I shouted. 'Let's hear from Myra. Myra Gaines and her unmovable husband. What about it, Myra?'

She raised her head. 'No,' she said. 'He wasn't making gestures to Andy. It was for me.'

'Now we're coming to it. It was for you, Myra, he was

making gestures. What was it supposed to prove, assuming the news got back to you by way of Paterson?'

Somewhere beneath the surface I'd stirred up a surge of memory, of contempt. 'That he wasn't a coward.'

'Did he have to prove it?'

'He had to,' she said. 'He had to prove something. I wasn't going to let him get away with it, sitting around and letting everything flow past him, not noticing...' She faltered.

'Not noticing you?' I asked.

'Not noticing.' The anger held her. She had quite forgotten the gun on her lap. 'I never loved ¦Andy. You're right about that. How could I? But it had to be somebody like that, somebody rough and overbearing. Neville was locked away inside his own shell. I couldn't live with a man like that. Just couldn't. You understand? He'd got to come alive, do something, show me...' She tossed her head. 'I told him about Andy, but he wouldn't listen. I showed him Andy, and he pretended he couldn't see. In the end I think he saw, but he was afraid. Neville was a coward. He couldn't face Andy. Not to go up to him and say look here I've had enough of this, or whatever men say. He was afraid.'

With her hands flying in over-emphasis, she angrily demanded my acceptance. I looked at her with the stony disbelief I thought Neville would have used. It worked. Her eyes were wild.

'I'd shout it in his face. "Neville, you're a coward." And he wouldn't blink. You could slap him, and he'd turn away. A rank coward. He'd just got to do something. I couldn't have gone on unless he'd done something. I think he saw that in the end. It was making me ill—the scenes.'

She stopped. She looked around. I'm not sure she knew where she was.

'Scenes?' I prompted.

'At the end, that was. He was stubborn, sullen. He'd sit for hours, not speaking, looking at me, and you could scream in his face: coward, coward. And it was like shouting at a wall. He had to do something. You *must* see that. Something for me. Not for Andy. That gesture was for me!'

Somehow Finn managed to force words between those lips. 'For you, Myra.' I looked at him. He'd have liked his fingers at my throat.

'Mother,' pleaded Karen feebly. 'You mustn't get upset.'

'I don't believe her,' I said angrily. 'Go on, Myra. Wave that silly gun. I don't believe you. Myra and her dramatics! Everything had to be for you. I can see you, shouting in his face: you're a coward. Feeble Neville, the useless nothing. So he went to all the trouble of finding Lovejoy in Birmingham, buying a gun, making clever conversation so that it got back to Myra! No, I don't believe it.'

Myra flashed at me: 'It was for me.'

'He'd got another gun, 'I reminded her. 'It was his own. He'd had it for years. So if he wanted to make gestures to *you*, Myra, why didn't he dig it out and wave it under your nose? Why didn't he do something like that?'

He triumph came out as a twisted, condescending smile. 'Because I'd got it hidden away.'

It had been a tiresome business getting to it, but now it was in the open. 'You'd hidden it away.' I sighed.

There was silence in the room. She raised her head. 'I wasn't going to make it too easy for him. Oh no. He'd got to go out and do something. Show me. Anybody can wave a gun. He'd got to *do* something.'

'But he searched?' I asked wearily, thinking of this great house we were at the moment sitting in.

Her laugh was so brittle that the hair on my neck tingled. 'The poor idiot. All over the house. Not letting me notice. Still pretending he wasn't caring. But I knew. It was the first sign I was getting through to him. Fumbling through drawers, upstairs and downstairs. It really was idiotic. You'd have laughed.'

So all right, I'd have laughed. The dull throb she gave in illustration had all the humour of a falling guillotine.

'It was for you,' I agreed. 'And that was what Karen tried so hard to hide. Sometime I was going to wonder why he'd go for another gun when he already had one. She didn't want me to think too deeply, so she gave me an answer she hoped would rest my mind—a gesture for Andy Paterson.'

Karen's face had sunken into hollows of despair.

'But of course,' I said, 'once he'd gone out and done something—bought himself another gun—there'd be no reason to go on hiding the first one. Let him have a real go at it. There were two guns used up at that farm. Ten shots were fired. The one he bought from Lovejoy was found in the yard, empty, and his own in the cow byre with three fired. But which was used first? That's the point. The three-shot gun hadn't jammed, so you'd think he emptied Lovejoy's first, then carried on with his own, fired three from that, and threw it down. But where did he throw it. Into the cow byre? He could have tossed it in through the doorway. But from his own statement he emptied Lovejoy's gun into Paterson, there outside the doorway, threw it down, and then ran off. It was found there.'

Finn croaked something. I ignored it.

'And it sounds so real. It's just what he would do. He went on squeezing the trigger after the gun was empty. That sounds very true. So what does that leave us? That he'd been using his own gun earlier, and discarded it after three shots? But why? It hadn't jammed. And anyway, it was found in the cow byre, and the chase didn't go that way—it finished there. So we've got to come to the conclusion that Lovejoy's gun was emptied first, and Neville's own gun was fired afterwards.'

Myra's eyes were like steel.

'But there was a letter from Paul Hutchinson's father,' I told them. 'It was stolen because it said something about the place the gun was found—yet in fact that was not the significant point in that letter. The important thing was that Hutchinson mentioned he'd found three shell cases in the cow byre. *Inside*, mind you. Now ... Neville could, conceivably, have tossed the gun into the byre. But he couldn't have tossed the shell cases. Quite simply, it means that those three shots, the three shots that must have been fired *after* Neville emptied Lovejoy's gun, were fired from inside the byre, where the shell cases were ejected. Are you going to say that Neville, having exhausted one gun out there in the yard, would scramble over Paterson's wounded body in order to fire three more from inside?'

It was a quarter to two, and I was very tired. Nobody said anything. I kept hammering at Myra.

'I don't think he ever found his own gun, Myra. You'd hidden it away, and I don't reckon you'd have made a poor job of it. In the end he was on the borders of insanity. He went out with the gun he'd got from Lovejoy. You'd finally driven him to something definite. But don't tell me you'd watch him leave, and not want to see him finish it. You hated Paterson by that time. You had to see it end. So you followed Neville to the farm, and you took along Neville's own gun, just in case it didn't end satisfactorily. You watched the hunt from the shadows, and when it got close you hid in the byre. So you were there when Neville emptied Lovejoy's gun and ran off. Then three more shots were fired. Why, Myra? Because Neville was a lousy shot, and Paterson wasn't dead?'

Myra said heavily: 'It became very heavy. I was wet and cold and tired.'

So she was cold and tired! 'And so immersed in yourself and your bloody rotten feud with Neville that you forgot Karen,' I said. Forgot her? Damn it all, this was the first time she'd given her a thought. I saw the horror come to Myra's eyes. 'Karen was here in the house. She was a child, and she'd watched it happening in front of her. Do you think she didn't see her father storm out of the house with that gun he'd got from Lovejoy? Don't you imagine she'd have watched while you found the gun you'd so carefully hidden? And then what? Her little scared face at the window as you drove after her father, that's what. So she *knew*. All this time she may have said nothing, but she's known damn well who killed Andy Paterson. It's a nice thing she's lived with, that and her father's hanging. I wonder if she's really loved you, Myra! Maybe she's just been tied to you by the shared secret.'

I watched while they turned their heads slowly to face each other. I don't know what it cost them. Then Karen collapsed, her hands over her face, and I felt like hell.

I had to look at Finn, because I didn't fancy the sight of Myra. 'You knew?'

He moved his tattered lips. It could have been yes.

'But you couldn't leave it alone, could you? You couldn't just sign me off and send me away.' He gobbled something. 'All right, you did what you could for Myra.'

I looked at her. She seemed numb, reaching back to Neville. I flapped at my pockets, as though seeking a cigarette, got up casually and opened the box on his desk, and on the way back scooped the gun from Myra's lap. She looked up at me. I think she was asking me for something, so I told her why I wasn't going to deliver.

'There was a time when I thought you were working for

Neville, keeping quiet about the fact that he owned a gun. But of course it was Myra you were thinking about, wasn't it, Myra? But Neville must have known. As soon as there was mention of a second gun, he knew, because it had to be the one you'd hidden. He fought hard for himself, but for you too Myra. There came a point when he could have saved himself with a few minutes of conversation with Crowshaw. But he kept silent. And you say he was a coward! You should count yourself as proud to have known him.'

It was the dull end of the night. I shrugged firmer into my jacket.

'And now ... if you'll excuse me.'

They all looked at me. I said: 'I'm getting married in a few hours, and there's a lot to clear up.' Then I picked up the phone and called Freer. Nobody moved. I laid the gun down on the table beside me.

'Mallin,' I said.

'Don't you ever sleep?'

'I'm hoping to,' I assured him. 'You'll have to get dressed. This matters.'

'It's broken?'

'Wide open. Can you come to The Beeches? Get over here as fast as you can.'

He was alert. 'Important?'

'Yes. You'll need some men and a couple of women officers. And a wagon. There'll be three arrests.'

'Three?'

'When you've heard it all. Oh, and Freer ...'

'Yes?'

'As a favour, make it fast, will you. I'm getting married in six hours' time.'

As he hung up he gave a laugh I didn't like. Finn was making croaking noises of protest.

'Yes,' I told him. 'Three. Don't think you're getting out

of it. There's Troy down there in the car. You ordered that, Finn. You probably did it yourself, while the others held him. No, don't say anything. He was the one who knew where the other Rover's gone, and he was the one who tipped Karen about Lovejoy. But that wasn't the worst. Oh no. He laid his hand on you, didn't he?'

God, I was tired. And there was half an hour before Freer could be expected to arrive. I filled the time by helping Finn a little. I helped him tell me where his cheque book lived. I helped him grab hold of a ball-point.

'Two hundred,' I said, 'should cover it. Two suits ruined, and a hell of a lot of mileage. Yes, two hundred.'

They're quite legal, I find, cheques with blood dripped on them. There could have been a tear on there, too.

When Freer burst in, I was just through phoning Elsa.

'David?'

'It's me, Elsa. Aren't you in bed?'

'Are you all right?'

'It's all over, love. You can rest now.'

'But are you all *right*?'

'I may not look too good, but I'm whole. Elsa, I've got to ring off. I'll see you later.'

'David, I love you,' she said.

'You too,' I mumbled, because three pairs of eyes were fastened on me, and they'd not want to hear about love.

Freer did his best for me, but we couldn't do it all at The Beeches. Nothing would do but all of us over at HQ, where I dictated a very long statement and had to sit for an eternity while somebody pecked it out on a typewriter in the back. Nobody was going to let me go on a honeymoon until it was all down on paper.

I signed my name a number of times, shook hands with Freer, who hoped I'd be very happy, and got out of there in broad daylight. I was a hell of a way from my place.

I made it in time for a bath, with my left arm in the air, and a shave and a scramble into the clothes I'd put out, just as Ted arrived with the taxi and my buttonhole in his fist.

'My God, you look rough,' he said. Ted's not as big as I am, but he makes up for it in intelligence. 'Didn't you get any sleep at all?'

I told him I hadn't. 'I'll make up for it tonight.'

'Good Lord!' He looked at me, appalled. 'We never did get time for that little chat, did we?'